P EW

PRIVATE VIEW

Meg Elizabeth Atkins

This Large Print edition is published by BBC Audiobooks Ltd, Bath, England and by Thorndike Press®, Waterville, Maine, USA.

Published in 2004 in the U.K. by arrangement with Robert Hale Limited.

Published in 2004 in the U.S. by arrangement with Allison & Busby Limited.

U.K. Hardcover ISBN 0–7540–7696–2 (Chivers Large Print)
U.K. Softcover ISBN 0–7540–7697–0 (Camden Large Print)
U.S. Softcover ISBN 0–7862–6033–5 (Nightingale)

The text of this Large Print edition is unabridged.
Other aspects of the book may vary from the original edition.

Set in 16 pt. New Times Roman.

Printed in Great Britain on acid-free paper.

British Library Cataloguing in Publication Data available

Library of Congress Cataloging-in-Publication Data

Atkins, Meg Elizabeth.
Private view / Meg Elizabeth Atkins.
p. cm.
ISBN 0–7862–6033–5 (lg. print : sc : alk. paper)
1. Art dealers—Crimes against—Fiction. 2. Police—England—Fiction. 3. Misssing persons—Fiction. 4. Art thefts—Fiction. 5. Large type books. I. Title.
PR6051.T5P75 2003
823'.914—dc22 2003061808

CHAPTER ONE

Not much happened in the life of Archie Barnes, art critic of the *Chatfield Argus* and occasional drama critic (and in that capacity once so reduced by the ineptitude of an amateur production he ignored the play and reviewed the interval).

In the years since his cub reporting days, when he had gone about his work by bicycle, he had learned to gauge the exact moment when the news potential of an event coincided with his boredom limit—then he left. This instinct almost failed him on the February evening in 1986 when he was preparing to leave the private view at the Minikin Contemporary Art Gallery but was delayed, searching for his hat. The paintings weren't bad, he'd seen enough to write his piece and would come back to enjoy them for himself another time in the company of the always welcoming proprietor and his excellent malt whisky. For the present the crush was keeping him from any enjoyment and he had had enough of shrill voices, Co-op Cava and frantic artistic posturing.

So it was that, instead of being ensconced in his favourite corner of the Waterloo Arms behind a pint of Chatfield's finest bitter, sighingly taking the weight off his feet, he was still at the Minikin Contemporary Art Gallery when the incident occurred.

The proprietor, Edward Minikin, known as Minim because of his diminutive size and high voice, was devoted to his artists: cherishing, encouraging them, assisting in their love affairs, passing on their gossip, even—when unavoidable—lending them money.

He made up for his slight build with Cuban heels, bravura hats, and flowing cravats, seeing himself as a dramatic presence forever poised on the edge of scandal and mystery, which he loved. In fact he was generally regarded as a really nice old queen, a bit *passé*, but at least a dash of colour in achromatic Chatfield.

The gallery was his passionate hobby. Everyone knew it was subsidised from his shrewdly managed private income but everyone nevertheless upheld the fiction it was a thriving, thrusting, cutting-edge (a term at that time coming into currency) venture essential to the artistic life of the city. So they always turned up in response to his invitations: friends, contacts, enthusiasts, dealers, hopefuls, all cohering into a rackety and amiable crowd. On that November evening the crush was larger than usual. This was accounted for by the unscheduled appearance of one of the most high profile art critics of the day, Dorian ffloyd.

As an old friend of Minim's—and fortuitously passing through town—Dorian ffloyd dropped in out of patronising loyalty and enjoyed himself posing elegantly and looking down from his six foot four vantage point at the inadequacies of the common ruck. He had made it known that this was a purely personal visit and he wanted no publicity. Minim, in enthusiastic agreement, telephoned everyone he could think of in the time available and casually mentioned the thrilling presence.

Fortunately, because the occasion was considered too small and hand-knitted to interest the media, its sole representative was Archie Barnes who counted himself glumly fortunate to be in the company of a person described by one of the many people who could not stand him as 'a long streak of poofter piss.' There was also an enthusiastic amateur photographer eagerly showing off the very latest in camcorders, directing his cherished equipment in every direction and capturing, in sound and vision, the dramatic incident encompassing a misunderstanding, high words, Dorien ffloyd's current partner and the hurtling contents of a glass of Cava. The wine splashed down the wall between two canvasses, slightly staining the frame of one while ffloyd, having stepped smartly out of range, responded instantly, worked by the puppet strings of his recognised persona. 'Throwing wine *and* a tantrum simultaneously. That is sophisticated behaviour for such an inept little shit,' he drawled, continuing—into a riveted silence—'Do you also have the mental capacity to grasp that in pursuit of your pathetic vanity, you almost damaged this outstandingly interesting work?' His hand, in a languidly significant gesture, indicating the picture with the wine dabbled frame.

He had exercised no judgement, it was doubtful he had given the work so much as a glance. He was concerned only with retrieving his foothold in a social landslip, with reinstating his superiority. It never occurred to him that, on what should have been a private and unremarked local occasion, he would be captured in print, voice and gesture—by means of Archie Barnes and the pitilessly enthusiastic amateur camcorder.

Archie filed his copy, the photographer had his delirious moments on late night local TV (later networked. After all, it *was* Dorian ffloyd) and the interest of the art world focused upon not one, but two paintings by a previously unknown artist called Fayne.

They were entitled, simply, 'Casement One' and 'Casement Two.'

Casement One showed a view from inside a church, or cloister, through the gaunt granular of a gothic arch. Two tall, narrow lancets with a central quatrefoil, solid, almost crude. On the inside window ledge stood a candle and an open Bible with an elaborately embroidered marker. There was an equipoise: the soaring simplicity of the window itself and its watch upon the harsh workaday landscape of fields back-breakingly tilled. Not a single figure animated the scene and yet there was a breathing reality of poverty-driven lives whose only salvation, if it could be grasped at all, lay in a vision of pious certainty.

In Casement Two a French window opened on to a view of a tennis court, its surrounding shaved lawn, luxuriant shrubs and artistic plantings of flowers. In the shade of a willow, exquisitely al fresco, stood a lace covered table set with a jug of lemonade, tall glasses; at the vanishing curve of the driveway an Armstrong Siddely was parked. As in the first painting, no human figure appeared and nothing was shown of the interior except the low window ledge beside the open French window on which stood a slender figurine of the cherished Art Deco dancing lady, head tilted back, delicate arms holding out the upward sweep of her long skirt.

These two pictures, identically presented in unobtrusive dark frames measuring eighteen inches by sixteen inches, were glazed and mounted, executed in coloured pencils on paper. They had in their delicate simplicity a haunting quality: the sense of time suspended, of presences just fled.

Minim was enchanted with them, with himself, with the entire evening. He was carried forward on a tide of publicity he had not engineered: chance had brought him not just increased business but exposure for an unknown artist. He delighted in the mystery, hinted at a special relationship with an exceptional talent.

He did not look beyond the immediacy of the situation, could not know that its ripples would spread far beyond Chatfield, out into the art world and the snapping jaws of the media, lead later to murder and afterwards take DCI Sheldon Hunter to the market town of Rush Deeping and another death.

* * *

The two Casements, moderately priced at £350 each, sold promptly to a Texan millionaire who was besotted by all things English. During the following two years, three more appeared.

Casement Three was a view through a cottage window of a crowded garden where vegetables and flowers intermingled; on the edge of the picture stood the glanced section of a brick outdoor privy. The room looking on to the garden could only be what was once called a scullery. Old fashioned domestic implements on the windowsill: a colander, a wooden spoon, a dish mop. This was a view of a world comforting in its continuity, yet there was something narrow about it: the squinting suspicion of anything new, anything changed.

Casement Four looked on to a narrow, industrial street, a terrace of poor houses dignified by the evidence of an unending war against grime: donkey-stoned steps, Red Cardinal windowsills, cheap lace curtains sparkling white at polished windows. On the windowsill a rent book, a miniature cup and saucer that declared itself *A present from*—the name turned from sight.

Casement Five looked down to the toppling roofs and chimney pots of the stacked houses of a small seaside town as it descended to a curving bay. On the windowsill stood a collection of shells, a ship in a bottle. This picture, unusually, was bright with a sweep of yellow sunlight, a clarity and blue distance in which there was something of all childhood's reprise of a cherished holiday.

These three, carried on the tide of popularity, sold at once. Casement Three went for £600 to a rock star; Four was bought for £900 by a Cheshire-based philanthropist who believed that native talent should stay where it belonged and donated it to Chatfield City Art Gallery.

Casement Five went for £1,200 to an antiquarian book dealer who collected artwork of any kind relating to his passionate interest, the English seaside.

But in all this time, no one knew the identity of the artist.

It was Minim's glamorous secret. Being

Minim, as all who knew him appreciated, this was not a commercial, money-spinning venture. The increasing value of the paintings was neither his doing nor his satisfaction. Although he had enough business acumen to be grateful for a jolly good profit, what counted for him was that he had centre stage in his very own drama. And amongst those who knew him very well, there was the assumption that in his deep kindliness he was helping out an artist who had to be in God knew what straits to remain concealed behind Minim's elfin guard.

And then—the latest, Casement Six.

To crank up expectation, the rumour spread that the artist himself would be present on the evening of the private view. It was no good asking Minim. Delighted as he was at the dissemination of any rumour—especially this one, which no doubt originated with him—he simply refused to say anything sensible and performed paroxysms of hand and eyelash fluttering.

Archie Barnes attended the occasion. After all, he had seen the beginning, he was virtually on the eve of retirement, and so found an almost poetic harmony in the likelihood his last assignment should coincide with the appearance of the elusive Fayne. The rumoured appearance. The possible appearance.

The eventual non-appearance.

Casement Six caused furious comment. For

one thing, it had a title, as the others had not. It was called *The Man in the Fog*. And it had figures.

From the window (of course, the window) the back view of a man receding, dissolving into a mist-hung background, blurred and indecisive.

The suggestion of foliage, a path, a gate. And then, within the room, for the first time, a section of interior so dark there was only faintly discernible the seated figure of a woman, her face turned away from the viewer, towards the window.

After the private view the painting *The Man in the Fog* disappeared from the gallery.

And on that night, Minim was murdered.

CHAPTER TWO

It was raining. Relentless, end-of-the-world rain. Dark, and cruelly cold.

The alley that led from the main road was more of a chasm of locked back entrances, litter, clustered wheelie bins. Twenty feet down, half swallowed in the maw of racking ugliness, shone the lighted entrance of the Minikin Contemporary Art Gallery. Beneath its brave and colourful and touchingly sad awning, stood the unquenchable figure of community policeman, Constable George

Withers.

'Sorry about this, Sheldon,' he said. 'And God, what a night as well.'

'It's all right, George, can't be helped,' Detective Chief Inspector Sheldon Hunter murmured in comprehensive resignation. 'And you know what they say—a good downpour's worth ten policemen. So at least it'll keep the gawpers away.'

'Don't count on that. Wait till the circus arrives, nothing like flashing lights and patrol cars to draw the crowds. You'd think it was a bloody film premiere sometimes. But, look—your promotion—I was looking forward to a damn good piss-up.'

He had, in a sense, been serially looking forward to and celebrating it since they were boys together, fighting to keep their places on a seething council estate. Sheldon—younger, streakier, narrowly intent on his future—had never disappointed him. Always two steps in front, then three, then four.

On this drenching, icy night in central Chatfield they confronted each other with all the philosophy of professionalism and unassailable friendship: George, the epitome of the community policeman, measured, comfortable, fulfilled by his family life; and the groomed and powerful Hunter, newly promoted to Detective Chief Inspector.

'I was on my way home from the Clay Lane Estate meeting to change for your do,' George said, 'and this feller rushes out, grabs me, shouting about murder—police—ambulance—'

'That him?' Hunter nodded towards the small lobby where a white-faced man sat on a chair, huddled, aghast.

George spoke in a low voice. 'Friend of Minim. Poor devil, he's in a hell of a state. Only place I could put him.'

The man looked helplessly past George at Hunter, as if seeking comprehension in a suddenly lunatic world. Regulations demanded the scene of a crime be sealed off until CID arrived and it was typical of George that, having no other means to hand, he should do it with his body. His humanity would not allow him to let a man who had looked upon his murdered friend stand in an alley in the pouring rain.

'Friend?' Hunter queried.

'I know what you're thinking . . .' Of course he did, they had shared so much over so many years, in spite of their difference in rank, all too often words were superfluous. Hunter had no need to point out that harmless, ridiculous, good-hearted Minim—even given his habit of picking up rough trade—forever remained too naïve to know how dangerous friends could be.

'No. Genuine, this, they go back a long way. Seems there's been some kind of do on tonight at the gallery and when it was over, and everyone had gone, this special lot went off to their supper—booked at that arty-farty place—Fellini's, you know. They expected Minim to follow. When he didn't, this chap—Roddie Elliot—came back to see what was keeping him, found the door unlocked, went to investigate. It's really bad, Sheldon. It's no wonder he's collapsed.'

Hunter went to the man, put a hand on his shoulder and talked to him, compassionate, unhurried, knowing his words would swim in and out of the man's shock with little comfort and less meaning but leave at least a particle of calm. Then, with a gentle, 'You'll be all right here with George,' he went through the glass doors to the gallery.

It was neutral coloured, skilfully illuminated by recessed lights, softly carpeted; his large, raincoated bulk invaded it like a wet dog in a lady's boudoir. He paused, hands in pockets, looking around with his slow, assessing gaze.

Disorder: canvasses awry, fragile chairs overturned, leaflets scattered, a vase of flowers smashed. Blood: its ferrous smell, its smears and jets—a ghastly distortion of modern décor—all over Minim's preciously cared-for haven. And there, in a corner, Minim's slight, crumpled body. He had been attacked from the front, his face, neck and chest a mess of blood. It was obvious, even from where Hunter stood, that his hands, raised in a futile effort at protection, had been shredded.

Underscoring this grotesque act of rage and cruelty, a pitiful statement of Minim's forgivable human vanity—his wig—parting company with him in death as he would never have allowed in life, lying beside his body like a small, faithful animal.

*   *   *

The police surgeon had been and gone, it was time for Minim to go. He had always delighted in histrionic entrances and exits. Now he made his last exit, carried away in a body bag, while purposeful activity swirled around his despoiled, loved gallery, and the empty night outside erupted with noise and movement and lights.

The gallery was made up of a large square room opening on to a long, narrower room; doors opened off to an office, a cloakroom and lavatory. Hunter roamed everywhere slowly, consideringly, not searching for anything specific. It was possible, by no means certain, that something beyond his attention, something he could neither define nor explain, would bring about the merest shift of perception, there and gone, and only later would he come upon it embedded in his consciousness, and understand its significance.

DS Graham Hacket, who had arrived immediately after Hunter, had gone straight away with two uniformed constables to Fellini's restaurant where Minim's friends were gathered, waiting for him and their dinner. 'They had a hell of a shock when I told them. We're getting as many details as possible, Bale and Robinson are still at it, but nobody's making much sense at the moment. And it's going to be a long haul—this place was bursting at the seams earlier on, I don't know if it'll be possible to trace everyone.'

Hunter asked, 'Did anything happen during the evening? A quarrel? A scene?'

'Not according to them. You know that lot, everything-marvellous-darling. Bit of a let-down this special artist didn't turn up, the whole shindig was in aid of his latest painting—er—Casements?'

'You mean Fayne?'

'Yeah, that's the name. You know about him, guv?'

Hunter nodded. He'd seen Casement Two in the City Art gallery, come across articles in magazines. There had always seemed to him a private anguish in Casements: views from an interior world. And in the sound of the name itself: Fayne. Its archaic use: *I would fain . . .* A whispered yearning for something ungraspable.

'Bit peculiar, isn't it? No one seems to know who he is, but everyone was expecting him. But if that's the state of play, how would they know whether he was here or not?'

'You mean his latest painting's here?' Hunter gazed round at the exhibits, walked into the other room, back again. Now that he was alerted he could trace the fleeting intuition: the lack of balance in the meticulous arrangement. On one wall, something missing. That was where it had been, that crying space. 'Casement Six by Fayne,' Hunter said quietly.

Hacket consulted his notes. 'Let's see. Yep. Fayne. It was called . . . *The Man in the Fog*.'

'It's not there.'

'P'raps it's been sold.'

'Didn't Minim have an assistant—secretary—something?'

'Yeah, part-time assistant, Ms Jonquil Prendergast.'

Hunter would have accused him of making it up had he not known that Graham Hacket was incapable of making anything up.

'—pretty weird-looking but sensible enough, even though she's in a hell of a state of shock. Thought the world of him. You know how it is—until she can take it in we won't get anything sensible out of her.'

'Couldn't you get anything at all?'

'Only one thing, for what it's worth. She said Minim took a phone call about six-thirty—this shindig only ran till seven. It struck her as a bit odd at the time.'

'He didn't obligingly tell her who it was? No, thought not. Why odd?'

'She couldn't say—just that it was.'

'Could it have been Fayne, calling to say he'd changed his mind, wasn't turning up after all?'

'No. She thought it might be that. But when she asked him, he said no. Of course, he wouldn't want to disappoint the punters, so it's likely he'd keep it to himself, but she doesn't believe he'd lie to her, he'd have no reason to—he could have told her in confidence and could trust her not to say anything.'

'Right. Well, better get on to BT and find out where the call came from. If it means anything at all.'

It was traced to a public call box on the outskirts of Rush Deeping, a market town twenty-two miles from Chatfield.

CHAPTER THREE

When he interviewed her, Jonquil Prendergast's first words disconcerted Hunter, 'You knew Minim, didn't you?'

'Very slightly. Mostly by reputation.' Not knowing if she was aware of it or if, at the present moment, it was something to be gone into. She was an intimidatingly large lady wearing an assortment of bright clothes, her hair arranged in tight constructions of plaits, her voice the pure diction of hunting Cheshire. 'Ms Prendergast, we have no way of knowing, at the moment, if Mr Minikin's murder was connected with the artist Fayne and the removal of the latest Casement. Anything you can tell us will help.'

'Whatever I can do,' she said firmly.

'Well, for a start, did you know the identity of Fayne?'

'No, I had no idea, as I've already explained to your men, Chief Inspector. And I couldn't begin to guess, particularly in these circumstances.'

'But as Mr Minikin's assistant, I presume you had access to his papers—wasn't there some documentation? I have to admit I don't know how things work in an establishment like this. Contracts, agreements, accounts . . .'

'Anything more than petty cash, his accountant is the man to see, I can give you his address. Records, agreements . . . you'll find those in efficient, commercial outfits. Minim was neither.' She hesitated fractionally. 'Artists generally supply a curriculum vitae, but not invariably. And in Minim's case he relied a great deal on memory, on—his contact with his artists was personal—sympathetic—he was the least businesslike man, generous and—*who could do such a—*'

She stopped completely, looked away, blinking.

She wasn't a formidable, odd-looking employee, she was a nice woman, bewildered and grieving, trying to behave properly. 'You were fond of him,' Hunter said gently.

'Everyone was.'

Not everyone. Someone hated him so much

they stabbed the poor little sod to death.

'Such a dear. Thoroughly good sort. Heart of gold.' She took out a handkerchief, had a vigorous blow, said, 'I'm sorry, this isn't getting us anywhere is it?'

Hunter smiled. 'Well, let's look for somewhere to start. What you're telling me is that nowhere did Minim have the name or address of this artist, his telephone number, details of sales he had made.'

'That's right.'

'And that's usual?'

'No, no, not to that extent. Minim could be casual, absent-minded, sometimes. He wasn't a fool, but he was—unworldly. It's hard to explain without making him sound an absolute prune, but he loved mystery, drama. And he was frightfully loyal. He had a very special friendship with Fayne, he told me this when he took the first two Casements, on the last minute—'

'Sorry?'

'Well, an exhibition doesn't just happen, it's planned, sometimes a year in advance, if it's a big one. Minim's weren't like that, but they did require forward thinking. Who would exhibit, how the exhibits would be arranged, advance publicity, all the practicalities. Even for these modest shows there was work to be done. Fayne's first two Casements—Minim brought them in himself, the day before the exhibition, rather sprang them on me.' In her wisp of a smile there was a world of affectionate recollection. 'He said to me, "This is someone very, very special, Prenders, someone who needs help. Don't ask any questions, there's a sweetie. My lips are sealed." Well, I knew better than to try and get anything else out of him.'

'He'd just bought them, and turned up with them?'

'Sometimes he did buy work outright, or it was sale or return and he took a commission. He told me he had bought these.'

'Did he mean the paintings were special?—or the artist?'

She was momentarily disconcerted. 'Strictly speaking, they're not paintings, although that's how they're referred to. Actually they're coloured pencil drawings.'

'You mean—like crayons?' Hunter said incredulously.

She smiled, 'That's a bit misleading, isn't it—on a par with kiddies' pictures. No, these pencils are water-soluble. They allow the artist to achieve the finest details, they've been accepted in fine art for quite a while. As for Fayne's artistic ability . . . Quite workmanlike, but nothing special, his composition was a bit rigid, in his later work you can see his technique has loosened. No, the first pair were oddities—and people often go for them. A matched pair, too. Can be another selling point. But honestly, if it hadn't have been for the fluke of that utter boil Dorian ffloyd calling attention to them . . . there'd never have been a Casement phenomenon. Well, that's my opinion. Not that I put it in quite those terms to Minim.'

'Do you think it was his opinion, too?'

She thought. 'Maybe. But I told you, he was so loyal. You see, he rather liked to think of himself as a latter day Paul Durand-Ruel—' Hunter's blank look prompted her to explain. 'He was the man who fostered the Impressionists in the late eighteen hundreds. No, nobody could claim Fayne was in that league, his work was competent enough, pleasing . . . I don't want you to think, Mr Hunter, that Minim was passing off stuff without merit, just for a profit.'

Hunter shrugged. 'Your world's a closed book to me, Ms Prendergast.'

'Yes. Well there are plenty who do that, believe me, but not Minim. And he was so pleased for Fayne. I got the feeling there was something special about him; he was somebody who deserved some luck, something decent to happen. And Minim did say, oh, quite a while ago, that I'd meet Fayne, that we all would. And, you may know, he *was* supposed to be here for the latest . . .'

She stopped, produced her handkerchief again.

'You said, in your statement, that the latest Casement was different.'

'Yes.' She explained how it had a title, that there were figures. But what made the work striking was the different treatment, the total lack of clarity or detail. 'There was so much in shadow, indeterminate, the blurred figures, one receding, the other so *still*. It had a haunting effect, disquieting . . . And then, stuck to the back of the frame, was a small printed label with some lines from a poem.'

'And that wasn't the norm?'

'Heavens, no, most unusual. Dashed if I know what they were. The phrase "man in the fog" occurred, I do recall that because, of course, it was the title of the work.'

Something she had said caused his mind to shift gear. Frame. He asked her if it was common for artists to be so secretive. She smiled and said not obsessively, but they were very individualistic and some were isolated, often from choice. But, he persisted, surely there were necessary contacts with their profession—materials, for instance.

'Yes, but there are plenty of good suppliers in all large towns—'

'It was the frame I was thinking of.'

'Ah, yes.' She was quick to follow him. 'But Minim had his own framer, it was one of his idiosyncrasies. He conferred with the artist, of course, but he much preferred to take work unframed.'

'Right.' Another dead end. 'Could it have disappeared that night simply because it had been sold and the buyer had taken it away?'

'Oh, no, house rule. Minim kept sold work for the whole exhibition—this was entirely in the interest of the artist. Customers could come and enjoy the work even though it had been sold.'

'Bit hard lines on work that hadn't.'

She gave him a small, conspiratorial smile. 'There you have it, Mr Hunter. As you no doubt know by now, a red dot signifies a sale. It can be a bit like a measles outbreak . . . one spot, then quite a rash . . .'

'But not necessarily a genuine sale.'

She looked hurt. 'Minim did it for his artists, he could not bear them to think they'd failed. It's enormously important for an artist to get his work exhibited, and when it didn't sell . . . Minim returned their work so sympathetically, with words of encouragement.'

'But Casement Six was sold?'

'Oh, most definitely. To Sir Arthur Ramsbottom.'

'He bought Casement Four, didn't he? Gave it to the City Art Gallery.'

'And that's where this one was intended. Companion piece. He definitely didn't remove it. He's in the Bahamas. He'd have collected it on his return and had it installed in City Art with all due ceremony.'

Hunter asked her about the phone call. She said she was sorry, she wasn't in the office when he took it—'and he didn't say who it was, but—'

'Yes?'

'He went rather quiet for a little while. Only someone who knew him well would have noticed that something had made him—sad. But who . . .' She shook her head.

'One more question, Ms Prendergast. Could Minim himself have been the artist?'

'Good grief, no. Even Minim couldn't have invented an entire set-up like that. And as for his artistic ability—that really *was* kiddies' crayons.'

*   *   *

Hunter took himself off one day to the Chatfield City Art Gallery. Months, sometimes a year went by between his visits. He went there in search of a deliberate dislocation from a world often mad with frustration and squalor and disillusion. The permanent collection was an old friend, sometimes he contented himself with that, by-passing any visiting exhibition. If it did not always refresh his spirit there was space for the possibility that it might, and always, surrounded by the timeless and mute, wandering through familiar rooms, he was comforted by the gentle ordinariness of the smell of polish, the stone balustrade of the staircase cold against his hand, echoing footsteps, hushed voices.

And then, Casement Five . . . He knew that

street, all those streets. Embedded in his consciousness, acute, tender, they lingered like unfinished business in the interstices of memory. Whoever painted that picture had walked down that street as surely as Hunter himself.

The assistant curator, a jolly young woman, restraining her natural ebullience, murmured with genuine sympathy about poor Minim, what a sweet little man, so friendly, so genuine. 'You get a lot of poseurs in this business, Mr Hunter, you can't imagine.'

He didn't need to, he'd already met more than enough of them.

She said, 'You know *The Man in the Fog* should be here, as a companion piece. I never got a chance to set eyes on it. You don't think it had anything to do with his murder, do you? I mean—the coincidence of *The Man in the Fog* disappearing the same night.'

Hunter, ever wary of coincidence, murmured something non-committal.

'This is a bad business. I was hoping you might be able to shed some light . . .'

'Oh, if only I could, for Minim's sake.'

Afterwards, for a quiet, considering time, they sat in her office, drinking coffee and looking through illustrations of all the Casements. She talked about them at length, she was an enthusiast, tempered with Ms Prendergast's professional objectivity. At last she asked in a small voice, 'What do you think,

Mr Hunter?'

'I think whoever did these drawings had no place, belonged nowhere.'

It was the answer to a question she had not asked, but she nodded and said softly, 'Yes.'

* * *

Over the following months hundreds of statements were taken, hundreds of interviews conducted. Tentative leads were followed to vanishing point, the Home Office large major enquiry system—Holmes—became crammed with data that refused to form a pattern or indicate a motive. The investigation proceeded in and out of so many cul-de-sacs Hunter observed, 'We double back one more time and we're strangulated by our own hernias.'

It could only be assumed that the persistent vulnerability of Minim's personal life was the major factor in his murder. He had always managed to keep his professional and intimate life separate, but he'd had some bad patches: menaced, assaulted, robbed. He had never brought charges. He knew too well how the sad helplessness of his yearning for excitement could be instantly reduced to an episode in a local nick, halting explanations made to taciturn and cynical men who had heard everything there was to hear from pathetic old queens.

The time came, as Hunter knew it would,

when Superintendent Garret said, 'It's no good, Sheldon, in spite of everything, we're no further forward. Time we dismantled the incident room.' And Hunter, reluctantly, had to agree. It was maddening, improbable, that in the middle of a teeming town (true that on a soaking night people would not loiter) one, two—how many people?—had come and gone, murdered a gentle and well-meaning man and left no retrievable trace. And if there was an innocent explanation for the disappearance of the picture that had been the centrepiece of the evening, why had it not surfaced?

Enterprising journalists had revisited the Dorian ffloyd incident at Minim's that had sparked off Casements. In all the satisfaction of his provocative persona Dorian ffloyd stepped back into the limelight, deeply saddened by the tragic death of a dear friend and with absolutely nothing relevant to say. General interest dwindled, died. In the art world, legends and rumours about the disappearance of *The Man in the Fog* lingered with the persistence of all unanswered questions.

After a while there was even doubt that it had ever existed.

CHAPTER FOUR

The funeral service for Joseph Saddler was held on the eighteenth of March 1989 in the church of St Leonard's in the parish of Rush Deeping, Cheshire. He was eighty-three years old. In his lifetime a vast man, so reduced by five years of crippling ill-health that people who had not seen him in that time marvelled he could fit into a coffin of conventional size.

His widow, Violet, was short, well padded, with a countrywoman's apple-cheeked face. She was seventy-three, but had been born elderly, marching through the years with all her fossilised attitudes, beliefs, judgements, conduct. She could bear the weight, she was a strong woman, forty-two years of marriage to Joseph had seen to that.

She responded to condolences—as she responded to every social interaction—impassively. *Violet . . . Mrs Saddler . . . so sorry . . . how brave . . . at rest now . . .*

'He had a full and useful life; he was with his family at the end.' There was a suggestion, somewhere, that she should be congratulated. If she attempted the modulation of grief, it eluded her. Her voice penetrated, toneless.

'Of course he was with his family. Who else would have the old bully?' a woman muttered to her mother, who had been a childhood friend of Joseph's. 'And that's not entirely true. He was in that nursing home the last three months because he was completely incapable. Not that one can blame them, he must have been the world's worst patient. But Violet wouldn't let him dare breathe his last till they were all round him, in suitable attitudes of farewell.'

A gentle gaze. 'Darling, his children have lost their father.'

'Yes, yes, I know.' *With great relief if anyone told the truth . . .*

The Saddlers had married late; Violet was thirty-two when her first child, Adelle, was born. Adelle had nothing of her parents' build, she was tall, with fine bones that gave her an air of controlled nerviness; she was, as always, elegantly dressed, without any kind of show. Her well-formed face was as expressionless as her mother's. Occasionally something escaped, when she was with friends, or with strangers who knew and expected nothing of her. Now, no one would have been able to tell she was simply fed-up, that she would rather be anywhere else. But she had to do the right thing—be seen performing this ritual because, in common with the rest of her family, she cared inordinately what people said. Unlike her family, she did occasionally give thought to other people's feelings.

Her sister Margo, at thirty-six younger by four years, was a pared down version of her father, over generous in frame, gesture and voice; she had a voluptuousness, an aura of just-controlled sexuality missing in her mother and sister. Her brown hair was abundant, her lips red and full, her eyes beady, darting in a large face. Apart from her smart black suit, strainingly tight, there was no indication she was mourning, her attention being taken up by her eleven-year-old son, Joey—as always threatening mutiny—and argument with her husband.

Her husband, Ron, slickly dressed, barbered, manicured, had the shrugging shoulders and sliding glance of the life-long cheat. 'You're his mother, can't you stop him saying he's bored in that loud voice? It's making a bad impression.'

'Yes, and everyone knows I'm not responsible. If you hadn't been an absentee father . . .'

They were fixed in a habit of public wrangling: lowered voices, which they appeared to think could not be overheard; the occasional comment in a raised, artificial tone; brightly sweeping glances at everyone, meeting no one's eye. Some people found it deeply embarrassing, others relished the awfulness.

'I'm getting upset,' their daughter, sixteen and overweight, said stolidly.

Her mother's commiseration was brisk. 'It's your age, Charmian, all girls your age are highly strung. I was.'

Ron muttered something unfortunately audible to his son who at once repeated it with coarse schoolboy loudness. 'Strung-up, Dad said, strung-up'd be better, Dad—'

Adelle bent down, whispered into his ear, 'A pound and not another word.'

'Two,' he muttered out of the side of his mouth, mimicking his father.

'Yes.'

He nodded. His aunt would pay him later, she always kept her promises, unlike his parents who voiced large expectations that mysteriously too often never came to anything.

'It beats me how you manage that,' Margo said ringingly. 'Considering you've never had any children of your own.'

'I bribe him,' Adelle answered quietly.

'You always make that joke. It's stopped being funny, if it ever was,' Margo said with dislike. She was supposed to be the cheerfully outgoing one who never failed to see the comic side. She was always put out when Adelle challenged her by making a joke, even a failed one.

Violet stood by, so unconcerned nothing at all might be happening. She bribed Joey, too, when necessary. It was her silent triumph over Margo, who was too stupid to realise. A triumph slightly reduced by Adelle's complementary subversion.

Violet and Joseph's youngest child, their son Ian, was not present. No one remarked on this, at least, not to the widow and her daughters.

The mourners did not fill the small church. Joseph had been an invalid for so long and for even longer had not had a social life beyond compulsory family occasions: weddings, christenings, funerals, even those, in his last year, had ceased. It was almost twenty years since he had retired from business life; friends he might have had from youth had diminished down the decades; the few who had survived brought now by stalwart and unheeding younger generations.

The Saddlers had always been uncommunicative, sustaining themselves. Emotionally, it would not have mattered to them if there had been only the immediate family there. Socially, it did. Joseph had to be seen to be respected, remembered, his passing a public matter. The Saddlers had once been people of account in Rush Deeping. Since the late eighteen hundreds up till the First World War they had bred, busied themselves, contributed, endowed, sponsored, served as governors, local and parish councillors, trustees . . . Imprinting themselves in all their rectitude on the history of the town.

But that was a long time ago, no one remembered now, no one cared—except Violet and her daughters whose joint legacy of property, money, and reticence imbued them with an air of impenetrable satisfaction. Violet had issued a surprising number of invitations to the service and to the house afterwards, it never occurred to her that anyone would pass up such a privilege. She was personally affronted when many people did.

St Leonard's was a place of elegiac beauty, hidden behind trees, surrounded by mossy, leaning tombstones with intricately crumbling carvings, its fifteenth century tower held together by ivy, measured by a massive yew.

But Joseph was not laid to rest there, surprisingly, since there had been a Saddlers' burial plot for a hundred and twenty years. He was carried in for the necessary obsequies and then out again for the drive to the Crematorium just outside Hambling. Violet said it had been his wish.

He was taken past the homely rotas in the porch: flowers, cleaning, mowing; the impressive gothic gold lettered list of previous incumbents amongst whom the name Saddler appeared, 1890–1892. (The brief tenure was accounted for by the Reverend Hereward Saddler's preference for adolescent boys, which proved too embarrassing for anyone to talk about, much less take legal action, and resulted in his being removed to another parish.) Then through the slumbering churchyard and the yellow stars of daffodils, between tangles of foliage and old table tombs.

When he was deposited in the hearse, Violet, Adelle and Margo stood together, looking on neutrally, silent in their web of complacency.

*   *   *

Longley House stood on the superior residential area of High Martinsgate, a rising and falling road that curved between massive chestnut trees just breaking into leaf with tiny frills of green so delicate they were almost transparent. All the houses dated from the late 1800s when most were built or occupied by men who had previously lived in Chatfield, close to the source of their livelihood, whatever that happened to be.

But Chatfield changed with changing times and with the booming industry of factories, mills, workshops, the slums seeped outwards. The soot and blankets of fog made the air unbreathable. Delicate ladies and sheltered children could not be expected to endure such conditions; families and servants were moved out, leaving grand, grimy houses to degenerate into tenements, slums, squats. The migration was made easy by the means that brought it about: trains. Comfortable trains with deferential staff ran regularly to and from any of Chatfield's three stations, carrying prosperous artisans and professional men from the villages and small towns of the surrounding countryside where they had built their residences in the sweet air.

From many choices, Joseph Saddler's grandfather selected Rush Deeping in Cheshire. The Saddlers were craftsmen, as their name denoted, makers of harness. With the coming of the railways an astute Saddler saw the potential and turned the family business over to making luggage. No matter how high their fortunes rose they maintained their narrow, workaday morality; they knew what was expected of them, carried out their social obligations with blighting rectitude, lived and died joyless and worthy. If there were ever aberrations, mavericks, they were contained within private institutions, their lives never spoken of, their partings never mourned.

Joseph's grandfather moved into Longley House when it was newly built. Over the decades trees and bushes had grown so high and close there was no clear view of it from the road, just glimpses and odd segments of something ponderous and stern in hard yellow brick. It came to be admitted in later years that it was the ugliest house on High Martinsgate. If the Saddlers were aware of this they never acknowledged it; their judgements were moral, not aesthetic. And they were contented with their distanced lot.

Given the conditions of the time it was something of an advantage to be one step back from the main course of life. But with their unyielding temperament, their gaze grew ever more narrowly suspicious on any who were other than themselves. Embedded in complacency, they evolved a family tradition of emotional isolation. Ostensibly they moved amongst their fellow men but their disinclination to communicate made them harsh and grudging not only in their outward relationships, but amongst themselves. Scandal, financial difficulties, setbacks—whispers of these internal tensions might seep out, but few people listened, that was the custom of the times.

Violet and Joseph had been ideally suited. She deferred to Joseph, but just as often confronted him. They shared intense disapproval of the modern world and dislike of other people. If they disliked each other it never interfered with their marriage. Discord sustained them: on his side anger and tyranny, on hers the immovability of self-righteousness.

CHAPTER FIVE

The driveway at Longley stood to one side of the house; it had a high outer wall separating it from the neighbouring house and on its garden side a dense range of concealing evergreens. The funeral guests parked on the wide, quiet road and walked up to the cramped, gloomy front porch by a curving path where forsythia and magnolia, just in bud, thrust out unpruned branches to snag at coats, threaten hats. What could be seen of the garden had the severity of municipal planting: square plots and straight lines, geometric arrangements of heather and early primulas.

The large house was inconveniently composed of many passages and sharp corners, small rooms with high ceilings and meagre windows. The furniture, ugly and uncomfortable, was the accumulation of generations and, along with ornaments, turned the rooms into obstacle courses of knick-knacks, fringes, beadwork, antimacassars.

No decorating had been done for so many years there was very little colour left anywhere, everything had merged into a patina of khaki and old string. Although Violet never found it necessary to apologise for this, she did explain, 'Daddy couldn't have workmen about the place, being so poorly.' Which was true and as she was accustomed to living in a subfusc world she found nothing objectionable in it.

While a queue formed outside, shivering in the bitter, bright day, too many people jostled in the inadequate hall. There was no one to take coats, those who knew their way around made for the cloakroom-cum-telephone room. More followed, cramming the small space, others milled uncertainly. The cleaning lady, Mrs Beddoe, carried a laden tray from the kitchen, butting into people, muttering unhelpfully, 'I've got to get *through*. Through.

There. That way. Look. Go *on*.'

'I've not been here since I was a child,' one distant cousin said to another. 'I'd never seen so much dark brown varnish in my life—it's *still here*—oh, God how can they stand it? What lovely old wood must be underneath.'

'Well, you know Violet and Joseph, never allow *anything* to be changed. Well, not much. They did go over to central heating finally. And they did put in a shower room near the old pantry after Joseph couldn't manage the stairs.'

The dining room and what had originally been the drawing room, but later generations of Saddlers called the lounge, were the only large rooms in the house. In both of them the furniture had been pushed back against the walls and an assortment of seating arranged in a circle, leaving an unwelcoming space in the centre. Bowls of hyacinths stood about, their cloying scent heavy in the chill air.

Here and there, in corners, the fugitive brightness of silver gleamed: cups and trophies. After Joseph had retired—shoe-horned out of the family business because of his refusal to move with the times—he suffered a mild heart attack, although how a man so unwieldy and splenetic could have anything mild was a marvel to people who knew him. He recovered, spent the later, active part of his life breeding bull terriers and aggressively competing at dog shows. Their photographs hung on walls, stood on every surface, their bulging faces and the glare of their small, dangerous eyes unnervingly reminiscent of Joseph.

The press in the hall became too much, people were forced to trespass into the two rooms, standing, moving about, anything to avoid the dauntingly empty centre, which nevertheless soon filled. In the dining room the long table had been moved into the bay window, it contained dishes of crisps and cheese straws and biscuits spread with meat paste and fish paste. There were trays set with glasses of sherry. Violet sat in a ponderously carved chair in the lounge, speaking graciously first to one side, then the other.

Adelle stood before the fireplace, warming her delicate hands, talking to her ex-husband, Trevor, who had good-naturedly come along to give her a little support; she seldom saw him. She had left the family home long before her marriage, after a university education strongly opposed by her father—'all this career business is no good for womenfolk'. She clenched her jaw on any argument, knowing it useless, and went her own way. She worked at the Department of the Environment in Chatfield as a statistician, a career that fulfilled all Joseph's rancorous prophecies because neither he nor anyone else could understand what she did. Her house was on the other side of Rush Deeping; she clung to the town, the life she had made for herself in it, she would not let her family drive her away but she lived as far from them as was possible.

In the dining room, Margo gossiped, and laughed. It was her habit, disconcerting to strangers and embarrassing to friends, to laugh frequently, without meaning or humorous context. Joey stood at the table, stockpiling food and eating ravenously at the same time. Margo said, 'Joey, put those sausage rolls back, there aren't many. And that slice of quiche. Charmian, do your social graces bit, take things round to people.' Charmian, huddled in a corner with young cousins, ignored her.

Mrs Beddoe continued to barge about with plates of scones and rock cakes, dumping them on the table and looking round triumphantly, as if daring anyone to help themselves.

Since no one else made the effort, Ron began to circulate, carrying a tray of sherry and a plate of savouries, his progress slowed to snail's pace by jokes and gallantries. 'How about giving your old Dad a hand,' he said jovially to Charmian.

She studied the plate he held with the concentration of the utterly self-absorbed. 'What's in these? You know how careful I have to be because of my allergies.' She took two handfuls of food and turned back to her cousins.

'Delicate little flower,' Ron said loudly, shrugging and smiling. He began to struggle round again, 'Mind your backs. *'Scuse* me. Food for the famished.' Two relatives, taking pity on him, picked up plates and drinks and began carrying them round.

Conversations threaded through the two rooms . . .

Social: *Yes, Margo and her family have lived here since Joseph had his stroke, five years would it be?* Well Violet couldn't possibly cope, and they'll be company for her now. *Do you think she'll stay on here? Houses on this side of town are still fetching very good prices.* Be better when this property slump's over, better to give herself some time, anyway . . .

Confidential: *Always trying to get his hand on your bottom, elbow pressed against your tit, ugh, right up until he was too ill to move . . .* D'you think Violet knew? *Every other bugger did. Avoiding Uncle Joseph was a family game we all learnt after we were sixteen.* Well, at least he had the decency to wait till then. *Mmm, I suppose. He certainly liked them pubescent . . .*

Critical: *Are these the funeral baked meats? Christ, I've scraped better stuff into the dustbin.* Why in God's name did Margo marry that smarmy sod? *Why d'you think? Best she could do.* And she was preggers . . .

Conspiratorial: *Doesn't anyone know what's become of Ian? You'd think he'd be here.* Why, for God's sake? They got rid of him when he was, what? Six? Shoved him on to Auntie Catherine at Chatfield. *Because Violet had that slipped disc and she couldn't cope.* Slipped disc. She had enough with the girls and Joseph wasn't going to tolerate another male in the house, threatening his supremacy. *I haven't seen Ian for years. Or any of them, come to that. And frankly, I can wait a lot more years before I do again . . .*

'Ron, didn't I see you and Margo looking at those new houses yesterday? The ones they're building on the market garden land. Executive what-nots. Surely you're not thinking of leaving this lovely old place? What would Violet do without you?'

'Tell you what, I'd no idea butlering was such hard work, fair wear me out, it will. Looking at—Whoops, there's Uncle Norman dying for another sherry. 'Scuse.'

Margo's current best friend said, 'Isn't that the woman who owns the bookshop? The one helping Ron. I didn't know you were related. "Rush" it's called, isn't it? Odd name for a shop.'

'Odd woman. Yes, Dorcas Grey. Second-hand Rose.'

'What?'

'It's what I call her. I'm always making up names for people, I'm famous for it. We've got a posh, *posh* cousin I've christened the Chinless Wonder.'

'But that's—'

'Yes, really funny, isn't it? Oh, Dorcas, she sells second-hand books.' Margo made her sound like a dealer in cast-off clothes. She had her mother's penetrating voice.

Defenders spoke up. 'Come off it, Margo, she has some terrific stuff—if you'd ever learned to read, you'd have found out. And she does have some new, as well.'

'Remainders,' Ron said. He had come across the word without any understanding of its meaning; it sounded suitably knowledgeable and derogatory. He read the *Sun*, racing results, and any magazine on the top shelf.

'So what's *wrong* with remainders? What's wrong with second-hand? I got a copy of *The Stones of Manchester* for a fraction . . .'

'I got a hardback of Graves' *White Goddess* . . .'

Other voices joined in: titles, authors; loved, respected, revered books.

Dorcas appeared with a tray of empty glasses. 'Margo, has the sherry run out?'

'Oh, probably,' Margo said. 'You might find some in the kitchen, though. Or maybe over there.' She nodded towards the sideboard, barricaded behind a row of chairs.

'I didn't know you were a relative,' Margo's best friend said to Dorcas.

'Distant, aren't you?' Ron said, winking.

'Not bloody far enough,' Dorcas muttered, going in search of sherry.

'Her mother,' Margo said, 'was some sort of cousin of Mum. To be honest, no one's ever worked it out.'

'Distant, like I said. Out of sight.' Ron laughed at his own witticism.

'And we haven't seen much of her till lately, she had a shop in Chatfield, sold it where that new development's going up. Must have made a mint. Then she bought one here. Lives over it.' Margo pulled a face.

'We used to live over a shop in Chatfield, when you left Dad.' Joey had turned up, unnoticed, to listen at her elbow. 'It was a laundrette. Grandma wouldn't let us come here, she said you'd made your own—'

'Joey, go and see if Mrs Beddoe wants anything carrying,' Margo said.

'She's going to buy a house. Auntie Dorcas. I heard her telling someone.'

'Strictly speaking, she wouldn't be your aunt. Would she?' Margo gave him a shove. 'Go on, make yourself useful.'

He wandered over to the table and began helping himself.

The current best friend was eyeing Margo with the increasing awareness of the duped. She had only recently moved to Rush Deeping and made no secret of being overawed by High Martinsgate and its grandiose houses. She knew scarcely anyone and had come to the funeral uninvited by Violet but pressed by Margo who was 'in need of civilised company.'

Margo's bounteous physicality and rowdy laugh misled people into thinking her a dynamic personality. A judgement reversed after short acquaintance with her repetitive vocabulary and blind self-regard.

She explained again, at length, about not seeing Dorcas since they were children, about the shop—'She came to see us when she was negotiating for it. Touting for business, I suppose. At least she had the nous to call Mum 'Mrs Saddler', not Auntie or Great-aunt, or whatever. Oh, no, Mum wouldn't have stood for that, not from someone she scarcely knows. I really can't be bothered to work out the relationship. Of course, if she does buy a house, it won't be up here, we won't be lumbered with her, thank God, a place like this is way out of her range.'

'It's certainly a revelation.'

'They are impressive, these grand old places, aren't they? Just right for this sort of occasion. Can't you just see all those stuffy Victorians gathered round for the reading of the will? Pity they don't do that any more.'

Adelle paused on her way to the refreshments. 'Why should they read his will? You know Mother gets everything.'

'Yes, well.' Margo laughed her inappropriate, crashing laugh.

'You know that very well,' Adelle said, with quiet persistence. 'Dad never singled you out. Oh, I know you've always been his favourite, but now that it's come down to it, Mother gets everything.'

‘What . . .’ Ron lingered, his baffled gaze passing between the sisters. ‘Margo . . . you said . . .’

‘She didn’t tell you she was in line for something special, did she?’

‘Joey, leave that food alone and go and see if you can help Mrs Beddoe,’ Margo said.

‘Ah, I see. She’s probably hoping to wheedle something out of Mother. Well, Ron,’ Adelle’s diction was precise. ‘You can put that right out of your mind. My sister has always been a great one for deluding herself, as you should—’

Dorcas paused in passing. ‘Adelle, several people haven’t had a drink yet. I can’t find anything in the kitchen except what Mrs Beddoe says is medicinal port and a bottle of some sort of health food drink.’

‘Haven’t you tried the sideboard?’

‘I can’t get at it.’

‘Can’t you? Oh. Ask Margo, I don’t live here, I don’t know where anything is. Wasn’t there a cocktail cabinet? In the lounge? Plays *Another Little Drink* when you open the doors.’

‘We took it to our quarters,’ Margo explained to the best friend. ‘We have our own lounge and whatnot, more or less self-contained, well, we can’t be under Mum’s feet with the kids—’

‘Why?’ Adelle asked. ‘You used to say it was in the worst possible taste. All that fifties cheap wood and coloured glass—’

‘Kitsch. It’s amusing.’

Dorcas said, 'Have you any suggestion about—'

Ron said, 'Your mother—' He was staring at Margo. 'You said it was more or less worked out—'

Ignored, Dorcas said, 'Excuse me,' and walked away while Margo hissed, 'Just drop it, Ron, now isn't the time.'

'Good God, it must be serious if you want to fight in private,' Adelle said mildly.

Half an hour later most people had drifted away. Dorcas, tired of reproachful looks, gave up the search for sherry, put down the tray of empty glasses, sighed, 'Sod this for a game of soldiers,' and went to make her farewells to Violet.

CHAPTER SIX

As Dorcas burrowed for her coat in the cloakroom, Margo appeared. 'Not going?' she laughed. 'Here, come and have a look at this set of Dickens. Just up your street.'

'Dickens?' Dorcas found herself hauled through a narrow, angled passage toward the back of the house. On this and on previous visits over the years she had subliminally registered not a book in sight.

'Been in the family God knows how long. Red leather.'

'Er . . . leather?'

'Something like that.'

They entered a large, littered room with a television, a massive table, rexine sofa and armchairs, a cocktail cabinet, 1930s tiled fireplace. The windows looked on to a concreted space, the remains of a stable with broken walls boarded up, and two asbestos garages.

'Our quarters.' Margo waved her hand about, talked at length of the many conveniences and drawbacks. Dorcas tried unsuccessfully to interrupt. The place was chilly and shoddy and depressing. After repeating everything twice, Margo said, 'Thing is, *sensibly*, Mother shouldn't hang on here. The house is far too big, eats money, and with Daddy gone, well. We've all agreed the sensible thing is for her to build a granny bungalow in the garden. Obvious, isn't it? Bags of space out there. We'll be on hand and she can have all the privacy she wants. Independence.'

'Well, that is important, old people often—'

'Exactly. Important. Thing is, persuading her. She can be stubborn.'

Margo chatted on, oblivious to the chill, concerned only with the granny bungalow. Dorcas glanced to one side, said involuntarily, 'Oh, how lovely.' In a corner, on a large white melamine chest of drawers, barricaded by trainers, videos, a radio, a satchel, a *Ficus benjamina* gasping its last, and sundry domestic items, stood a perfect doll's house. Every detail of its Queen Anne front was delineated, every pale rosy brick, every tile of its hipped roof. The dormer windows had intricately wrought pediments, the door canopy was carved in the delicate shape of a shell.

Dorcas's hands went forward involuntarily before she restrained herself from sweeping aside the rubbish that obscured it. How could anyone not long to swing open the front, to look into the secrets of its miniature interior life.

'Daddy made it for me,' Margo said carelessly. 'No kids here to play with it now. Full of furniture, he made that, too.'

'Your father? I had no idea he had such talent, he was, um . . .' Dorcas's few long ago memories of Joseph were of a shouting voice, a frightening figure, lumbering, bullying. And then the previous year, the vacant and helpless man in a wheelchair, as terrible in his collapse as the fall of some monolith. How could there spring from either of those men the patience and skill, the artist's eye, the craftsman's hands?

'We can't stand here all day,' Margo said impatiently. She opened a door on to a lobby, led the way to a small, coffin-shaped room lined with deep shelves. 'This would have been the library.'

'I rather think it was the pantry,' Dorcas said.

'What? What?' Margo glared. 'Look, our books are here—' as if that settled the matter. Every kind of clutter crammed the shelves; she rummaged. 'The kids' stuff gets everywhere. Honestly, this is supposed to be our shelf. See, Ron's engineering books.' She shoved them aside, not before Dorcas had glimpsed Hayne's service manuals, Glass's Guides, Cap's Guides. *Engineering books* . . .

'Here. The Dickens.'

It was the ubiquitous cloth collected works, Dorcas doubted no household in the country had ever been without one. She tried to explain, tactfully.

'Cloth?' Margo said with baffled indignation. 'Cloth, leather—what's the difference? They're all here. Just give me a price.'

'I couldn't, I'm afraid they're no use to me, so many were pub—'

Margo turned away. 'Oh, well, never mind. I can always get another opinion. Someone professional.'

She conducted Dorcas back briskly, apparently widdershins because they went into the dining room without encountering the hall. Violet was there, with Ron and the children, Adelle (whose husband had evidently made a prompt escape) and Uncle Norman and his wife Rose. He was a short man, an unmistakable thickset Saddler, with a puffy red face and beady eyes; Auntie Rose, presumably the effect of fifty years of marriage, remarkably similar. They looked like two garden gnomes.

Adelle held up a bottle of sherry, with a wry 'Ran this to earth.' She poured a glass and passed it to Dorcas. 'You've earned this if Margo's given you a conducted tour of the family junk.'

Ron hovered, shrugging. 'What about those valuable books? They're yours, aren't they, Margo?'

'Daddy said she could have them when she was a kiddie,' Violet said.

'You're never selling them, Margo?' Uncle Norman cackled. 'Oh, your dad wouldn't like that, he wouldn't like that one little bit.'

'She can do exactly what she wants with them,' Violet said placidly.

'I'm sure Dorcas appreciates their worth.'

Dorcas said, 'I'm afraid they're not—'

'It would be a different matter,' Violet steamrollered on, 'selling the doll's house. That's priceless.'

It wasn't. Enchanting and collectable—not priceless. But Dorcas wasn't inclined to offer an opinion.

'This food needs eating up, it won't keep,' Margo said, pouring herself a glass of sherry to the brim.

'Or the Saddler pearls,' Uncle Norman

persisted, leering at them displayed on Violet's bolstered bosom.

The value of the Saddler pearls was notional, no one had ever established the truth. It had long been whispered that a downturn in the family's affairs (1920s and 1930s unwise investments in exhausted coal seams, slumped ship building) had led to a surreptitious selling-off of valuables, including the pearls. One side of the family maintained that the fake necklace was later, in more fortunate times, redeemed. Another side insisted nothing of the kind—Violet was merely one in a line of Saddler women who went on, deadpan, wearing a string of worthless beads as if they were valuable. In ignorance or not, no one ever dared to ask, certainly not while Joseph was alive. The reserve of the Saddlers ensured the subject was never openly talked of, but it generated its own momentum, contributing decades of murmurs, gossip and disparagement to the contorted mythology of the family, which encompassed many unverifiable items.

'That set of Dickens,' Adelle said, with mild derision. 'You'd be lucky to get rid of it at a car boot sale.'

Joey sat at the end of the long table, eating everything within reach. 'Mum told Dad—'

'Where's Mrs Beddoe?' Margo asked.

'Mum, you haven't forgotten Tracey's eighteenth birthday?' Charmian said.

'It's next year, for God's sake,' Ron said, clearly helpless before female teenage imperatives.

'How could I?' Margo laughed and explained at length to Dorcas. 'You know Tracey Williams . . .' Dorcas didn't. No matter. She was forced to hear at length about this relative of some sort who would be having her eighteenth birthday at the home of her parents. 'The Gables, just between Knutsford and Clerehaven. A private hotel.'

'It's bed and breakfast,' Joey volunteered, ignored.

'All the younger set'll be gathering there. There's room for them all, a large dining room, and a lounge, and of course a bar, which seems so important,' Violet said with satisfaction. 'Well, we thought, the best thing for our generation—just turn the whole thing over to them, make their own entertainments.'

Joey said, 'Tracey and her boyfriend told her parents they wouldn't have any wrinklies.'

'Although what sort of entertainment,' Violet added, managing, without any expression at all, to convey doubt and disparagement.

Charmian said doggedly, as if it should be evident to a fool, 'We'll just be, like, doing stuff.'

Violet repeated this, tonelessly, slowly shaking her head.

Charmian said, 'Mum, I'll have to have

something to wear.'

Margo murmured yes, they'd go to Chester.

'Chester! Ugh. No one buys anything there.'

'I do.'

'That's what I *mean*,' Charmian said, serious, her face full of contempt. 'It's got to be Chatfield.'

'Oh, all right. I suppose I was just as fussy when I was your age.'

'The service did justice to your father,' Violet said complacently. 'Everything's gone off very well.'

Uncle Norman and Auntie Rose nodded.

'Oh, *very* well,' Margo agreed.

They all looked at Dorcas. What was there to say? Could a burial be cause for self-congratulation? 'Um, well, yes . . .'

It could not be that in her floundering she had said the right thing, she had not said anything at all, but there was, infinitesimally, a shift in the atmosphere, as if a tension had been relaxed, an obstacle subtly overcome.

'Aren't you Ernest's girl? Used to live in South Chatfield? Solicitor. Well, he was when he was alive.' Uncle Norman shook with silent laughter at his own joke.

Ron leaned closely to Dorcas; she was backed up against the table and had nowhere to go. 'Margo said those books should raise a fair bit.'

Dorcas had had enough. She said firmly, 'Dickens was a hugely popular author, he was prolific and had a long run. That means that countless editions of his collected works were published at a very low cost over a period of—'

'You're not going to tell me they're not . . . Ah, yes, I get it.' Ron smiled conspiratorially, nudged her. 'Can't kid one that's kidded thousands. Can't tell me anything about doing deals . . .'

She turned desperately to Adelle who, looking on with a small smile said, 'Oh dear, oh dear. Ron, I'm afraid Margo's been leading you up the garden path again—'

'Gardens, that's it,' Margo put her hand to her forehead in dramatic recollection. 'I knew there was something. It just went out of my head what with Charmian and all her fashion conscious image stuff. Kids are so demanding, aren't they? Attention-wise.' She gestured to the large window-framed view of the garden stretching away to the side drive. What might have been a prospect of openness and burgeoning growth was a moribund vista of rigid flowerbeds and dark *cupressus leylandii*. 'Space. As I was saying, and actually when I was just talking to Dorcas, she said what a good idea to build a granny bungalow for you out—'

Dorcas choked on her sherry. 'What? *I* said—'

'Yes, you pointed it out—*independence*. That's the important thing, Mum, you've always been so independent, that's what we've always said. And let's be honest, you can't cope with the children about you all the time. I mean, why should you? They drive me mad half the time, and you're a different generation, you can't be expected to adapt. Listen, Uncle Norman, wouldn't you and Aunt Rose, given the chance, choose to have your own . . .'

Arguments, objections, queries passed backwards and forwards amongst everyone except the children and Violet, who sat listening without reaction. Uncle Norman said, 'What's it got to do with her, anyway? Whosit? *Dorcas*. Was it her idea?'

Dorcas almost shouted, 'Listen, this has nothing—'

Margo said reasonably, 'Well, she's family, after all, she's entitled to her opinion.'

Adelle said, 'It's no good, Dorcas. Margo's decided to enlist everyone, she usually does when she wants to get her own way.'

'Yes,' Violet said, rendering all voices silent.

'What?'

'What? Yes, it's a nice idea.' Violet, as always, understated everything.

'Mum—do you—but—' Margo lost track.

'Of course,' Violet said imperturbably, 'I shall put everything in the hands of McGovern, our estate agent. They always handled our business when we had property to rent. I'll take their advice on the technicalities, what sort of permission we need. I don't see why we should go to the expense of an architect, a competent builder should do . . .'

They were all staring at her. Margo was the first to react, the project had engaged her and Ron since long before Joseph's death, she directed a passing glance of triumph at Adelle. 'Well, Mum, I must say, you won't—'

'—and anyone else necessary to see the whole thing well under way. Then I shall go and visit my sister in Canada.'

Adelle said faintly, 'Auntie Grace. But—but you don't like each other.'

'I need a break. It's been a strain coping with your father all this time. I shall go in the autumn and stay on for Christmas and New Year, and come back home in January.'

CHAPTER SEVEN

Violet had been away for two months when Margo received a telephone call from Canada. 'Hallo, Margo? It's Auntie Grace.'

'Hallo—' Margo laughed.

The only time Charmian moved with anything like briskness was when the telephone rang, then she materialised in all her solid and obtrusive reality. 'That'll be for me. Mum, is it? Who wants me? Mum, I'm expecting an important—'

'It's Auntie Grace from Canada.'

Charmian turned and plodded away.

'Hallo, Auntie Grace. What is it?'

'Well, it's your mother—'

Expectation leapt to Margo's eyes. She waited silently.

'You're not to worry, it's just that she's had a fall.'

'Has she?'

Grace, a true Saddler, expected nothing more in the way of response.

She went into details of accident, hospital—'She's going to be all right.'

'Good.'

'It's just that now she's going to be away longer than expected.'

'Right.'

* * *

Violet was away for almost a year, during which time she corresponded vigorously with her estate agent and architect about the bungalow, telephoned a constant stream of enquiries to Margo, issued instructions with the imperturbable assumption they would be carried out. When Margo discovered she was making frequent telephone calls to Adelle, she went round to Adelle's to find out what her mother had said and why.

* * *

The houses on Ruskin Close, smart, expensive, had been built just long enough to lose their look of being interlopers on old land; even in the sparseness of winter the gardens had the softened outlines of well-grown shrubs and trees. Adelle's house stood at the far curve of the Close. The front looked over the dipping road out to a side of the valley that scrambled up from the river Rush. As the foliage of the seasons went about their veiling and unveiling, sections of the town appeared, retreated: roads and houses and gardens, businesses and shops, spinneys and parks and public buildings. A friend, standing at her front window, once said, 'Your very own camera obscura.'

'What? Oh . . . Yes.' In her diffidence Adelle managed to suggest that this was a notion too exotic, but she hugged it to herself. After all the shut-in, quarrelling years at Longley House, where the light never seemed to reach into corners and rooms were full of her father's bullying voice, Margo's tantrums, her mother's prohibitions, it became a private triumph to her that she had reached an unassailable standpoint where everything was hers. Secure in possession of her very own camera obscura, she held the town in her grasp.

Margo always peered in at windows before knocking. The side gate was seldom unlocked, if it was, she would go through that, looking in all the windows, until she chanced on Adelle looking back at her. She would grin and wave; Adelle would glare. *Why don't you knock, Margo?—Why? I didn't think you'd be doing something you don't want me to see.'*

She drew a blank at the side gate, found nothing of interest in the lounge, stood at the front door with its shining brass fittings, pressing her face against the panel of reeded glass. Once, she had caught the blurred form of Adelle slipping into the downstairs cloakroom and enjoyed herself shouting through the letterbox, 'I can see-eee you. Hiding in the *toi-oi-let.*' Although Adelle, of course, denied she had been trying to do anything so childish.

Adelle opened the door, stood gazing at Margo.

'I can't stand here all day,' Margo said, and laughed.

Adelle held herself fastidiously aside, muttered under her breath, 'Take no prisoners,' while Margo barged in past the mahogany hall stand, a spindled affair she always seemed to be in danger of demolishing.

Apart from this delicate object everything in Adelle's house was plain and ordered and clinically clean, setting Margo's teeth on edge. She always claimed, 'I've other things to bother about than being obsessively house proud.' If Adelle was present she enquired coolly, 'Oh, have you? What?'

Margo said, 'Mum's been phoning you quite

a bit. What about?'

Adelle raised delicate eyebrows. What?'

'Well, I mean, has she said anything?'

'Said anything? What about?'

'I don't know.'

'Neither do I,' Adelle said with her cold, small smile.

The telephone rang. Adelle lingered, obviously torn between answering and leaving Margo free to roam her private space. The answerphone would at any moment advertise Adelle's private life to Margo's avid interest. It could be something trivial, it could be something Adelle wished to keep to herself. Wordless, Margo studied her, insolently, knowing, *Well, Miss Clever, now what do you do?*

Expressionless, Adelle went out to the hall to answer the phone, closing the door behind her. Margo blundered about the kitchen, opening cupboards and drawers, reading anything to hand: notes, envelopes, her button eyes darting. Furtively, she opened the door to the hall but Adelle was standing at the far end, speaking very softly.

Margo went into the lounge and contemplated Adelle's needlework. It was typical of Adelle to have a hobby that was silent and did not require creating a mess. She worked on large pieces of canvas that were stamped with coloured pictures of thatched cottages, country gardens or the occasional hunting scene. She patiently stabbed the required colours in and out of their minute holes and, after months of work, had the result framed and hung in the house, or made into cushion covers. She belonged to a group that met and sewed in one another's houses and went together to exhibitions and craft fairs.

Margo could find no sense in making something when it could just as well be bought. And when people admired her doll's house, she never said that it was Adelle, in those lost years of childhood, who had painstakingly measured and cut out, upholstered stitch by stitch, Joseph's much admired miniature furniture.

No one in the family ever remarked *why* Adelle had done this, certainly no one complimented her. Margo, being useless with her hands, never attempted it, Violet was much too busy; it was taken for granted that Adelle had nothing better to do. As far as anyone knew, although nothing was ever said, Joseph had never contemplated making a doll's house for Adelle. Her birth had brought shock to him that such a small being could demand Violet's time and attention with never-ending and voracious needs that involved sick and smells and noise. Violet was not maternal, but she knew her duty and Joseph, who was loud on the virtues of duty, found himself pushed into second place.

His ill grace simmered for four years; by the

time Margo arrived he had worked out how to get his own back. It was simple, direct and cruel: he punished one daughter with the arrival of the other. Margo was the cherished, desired, loved one, her every whim commanded attention; almost before she could speak she was in no doubt about her position and used it, crowingly, against her sister. Violet, dominating them both, never pacified or ordered, never raised her voice, never saw any reason to intervene in their fights, her response to the storms that raged constantly round her a placid, 'Serve you both right.'

Adelle came in. Margo said, 'I can't make out why Mum went to Canada, can you?'

'She needed a holiday after looking after Father for such a long time. It's perfectly understandable.'

'I need a holiday. I did the looking after as well, in case you've forgotten.'

'Yes, but you all went away last August, to Lanzarote. *And* the August before. Mother didn't. And you're going again this—'

'Well, I mean, all right, but why choose Canada? Mum's never had a good word to say for Auntie Grace.'

As Violet seldom had a good word to say for anyone there was really no constructive response.

Margo looked searchingly at Adelle. 'There's something going on.'

Adelle shrugged, edging Margo out of the lounge, towards the front door. 'Is there? You're the one who makes dramas out of nothing.' Margo, barging on, repeating: *Why Canada? Why Auntie Grace?* caught, in the hall mirror, the glance of a secret smile. When she turned, Adelle's face was as unreadable as always.

* * *

'Something's going on, I know it is,' Margo said to Ron.

'What?'

'I don't know. She's got that cat-with-cream look. Tries to hide it but she can't fool me.'

'P'raps she's got herself a boyfriend.'

Margo's laugh crashed, scornful, unamused. 'Who'd have Fat Ada?'

When she was particularly furious with, or out manoeuvred by, her sister, she reverted to the taunts of childhood. Adelle had shed her puppy fat late, tormented for years by the jubilant Margo: *you're fat, fat, fat. I'm only a kiddie, Daddy says kiddies are always plump, but you're grown up and you're fat, fat, fat.*

They had both grown up, changed places, but in spite of the physical evidence, Margo would never relinquish an advantage, however fraudulent.

And, beginning too long ago, beyond anyone's precise memory, Violet had said that

Ada was a common name—'Servants are usually called Ada.' Margo, old enough to understand a derogatory term, seized it, bestowed it on Adelle. Joseph was delighted by her cleverness. Violet left her to get on with it—and if it amused Margo as a kiddie there was no reason why she should not have her fun as an adult, and enlist her children. Without a restraining word, Violet continued to allow the next generation to refer to Adelle—a slim, professionally competent, independent woman—as Fat Ada.

Ron said, 'What can be going on? It's your imagination, don't worry about it. You've got enough on your plate seeing to the old girl's whims. We need to look after ourselves, that's the priority.'

It was. Margo's self-dramatisation had railroaded their life. When she was supposed to be a student of social science she was carrying on an affair with him; he was older, recently divorced—as she saw him, experienced and glamorous. She became pregnant, dropped out of university. Violet was not surprised; Joseph, furiously betrayed, for the first time turned his rage on Margo. The look of things demanded she be given a showy wedding, and Joseph put down a deposit on a house in Chatfield. In time he grudgingly allowed her to visit and bring her children, but he refused to allow Ron over the doorstep.

It was a fighting marriage: Ron's suspected infidelities, his questionable business deals, her inability to manage money; huge overdrafts, mortgage repayments ruinously overdue. After ten years and a volcanic row, Margo packed children and luggage in the car, telephoned her mother to announce triumphantly that she had left Ron and was coming home. 'Just a minute,' Violet said. 'Joseph, Margo's left Ron. She wants to come here.' Joseph had no need to pick up the telephone, he simply shouted, 'She married the bugger. He can keep her.'

Margo spent a wretched year, shifting herself and the children between one stop-gap and the next, carting them on furious confrontations with Ron, as public as possible. They never knew what to do, if they cried in bewilderment, she accused him, shrieking, 'Look what you've done. Look what you've done.'

Then Joseph had his first stroke. It happened at a time when the turmoil of Margo's existence overwhelmed her; she left the children with friends, fled to Longley to seek her parents' help—to find they needed hers.

It was a surreal reversal of roles and purposes, a trading of needs and favours, a crisis never specifically referred to again. The outcome was a collective reconciliation. For once Violet needed something from Margo, invoking Joseph's 'favouritism' of Margo. 'She always meant more to Daddy than anyone, in spite of everything. No one else could care for him the way he would want.'

Margo was efficient, matter of fact; she and Ron had decided to try again, for the sake of the children. Where better than Longley? After all, it was her home, so much space. 'And of course, I can be of use. Daddy's needs come first.'

Helpless and inarticulate, Joseph glowered a baffled rage, his small eyes boring into Violet, into Ron. When he began to regain a semblance of speech he swore at Ron; fortunately his words were so slurred no one could be quite sure what he was trying to say. A habit became established of speaking for him—so that he shouldn't overdo things. Margo was chief interpreter, frequently challenged by Violet, even the children joined in when they saw an advantage. Ron shrugged and smiled; visitors noticed most of Joseph's attempts were directed at him. Violet said placidly that Daddy appreciated having another man in the house. 'Extra pair of hands, every little helps, doesn't it? And family, too.'

Devoted care ensured his partial recovery; in time, he regained limited mobility, made hitting out motions that frequently sent proffered trays flying. Through sheer willpower, it was said, he progressed to a lurching walk with assistance and a stick. But when he began to hit out with the stick at objects, and even people, Violet decided he was overexerting himself, taking things too rapidly. She removed the stick. When Joey observed, 'It was only Dad he was trying to hit, mostly,' everyone pretended not to hear him.

Adelle's marriage had broken up in an amicable and diffident way two years before Margo's "reconciliation." Her ex-husband, Trevor, was the one person in whom she could confide who knew the family and was disinterested to the point of having nothing to do with them if he could possibly help it. Adelle said to him at the time, 'If you ask me, some pretty tough trading's gone on. No, I don't know what, and I don't want to know. They all seem to be satisfied. Mother, Margo and her ghastly family.' She shrugged. 'It doesn't concern me.'

'Still, when you think of it, it's magnanimous of your mother to give a home to Margo and her family—'

'Isn't it just? And that's exactly what she knows everyone will say. You know what my mother is about—power. She always fought Father for it, under the surface. Margo's too stupid to ever understand the dynamics of that relationship, she deals in easy victories. She's got Ron in Longley House and his debts paid off—everyone knew he was on the verge of bankruptcy.'

'Is that what you meant by trading?' Trevor asked uneasily.

'Of course, Mother's got everyone else doing all the work. And an entire family to dominate. She missed it when we'd left home, playing us off against each other. Now she can meddle to her heart's content.'

CHAPTER EIGHT

Violet wrote from Canada, *'I've been assured I'll be fit enough to return in time for you to go off on your holiday in Lanzarote. You don't want to miss it as you've held the fort all this time. As a thank you, have an extra couple of weeks away, at my expense. Enjoy yourselves. Adelle will move in with me while you're away, but I'm sure in a little while I'll be able to manage perfectly well on my own . . .'*

'She's beginning to appreciate everything we do for her,' Margo said positively. 'All the donkey work we've had with that damned bungalow. You'll see, she's beginning to realise, with Daddy gone and having that accident, how much she needs us.'

'She might have been a bit more generous,' Ron muttered.

Violet returned, walking with a stick, but vigorous and fit. Seeing them off, she reduced Ron to silence by handing them a lavish cheque, brushing aside Margo's thanks, 'It's the least I can do, after all . . .'

They returned a month later, sunburned, overweight—except for the persistently string-beaned Joey—with a compendium of souvenirs to add to the freight of junk in Longley House.

'Where's Adelle?' Margo asked. 'Isn't she supposed to be staying, helping you out? After all, that's what we agreed—we're away and she stays here—she's no *further* to go to work, for God's sake. What's her excuse? Selfish bitch, anything rather than put herself out.'

'Oh, yes, she did,' Violet said, unmoved. 'But after three weeks I found I could manage perfectly well if she just came in each day. She likes to be back in her own place.'

Margo said, 'Oh, well, yes. She always does. Still . . .'

'I don't need looking after,' Violet said. 'I can manage everything perfectly well.'

The lounge window gave a partial view of the granny bungalow; square, red-brick, it had been finished before Violet's return but builders' detritus continued to surround it like rocks in choppy sea. From its start to its completion it had never made the least claim to attractiveness, but nobody in the house would have noticed if it had.

'There's a car there,' Joey said.

'Don't make things up,' Margo said. The bungalow had its own small parking area opening off the side drive, not visible from the house.

'A red Metro. I went out and seen it,' Joey said.

'Saw it,' Margo corrected automatically. 'What's it doing there? Someone from the builders, or the estate agent, I suppose.'

'The new tenant.' Violet said, matter-of-fact.

The family stared at her. Joey volunteered. 'There's curtains. I seen them, too.'

'Shut up,' Margo said. 'Mother, what do you mean—new tenant?' She smiled weakly, in anticipation of an unlikely joke.

'I've let it. It has to pay for itself,' Violet said.

'But . . . you . . . you were . . . going to . . .' It was seldom Margo was short of words.

Ron stood by, stunned.

Violet thought for a moment. 'Going to what?'

'Live . . . move into . . . It's a *granny* bungalow,' Margo said.

'That's just a name, isn't it? No, I didn't say I'd live there. I took advice and found out it would add to the value of the property, so it seemed sensible to go ahead.'

'I don't understand,' Margo said helplessly.

'You said so often that I couldn't be expected to put up with having the children round me now they're growing up, and of course, you were quite right. I did a lot of thinking while I was away, and had Grace to talk things over with. There was no point in giving you more work, I got Mr McGovern to handle things for me. Just a six month let, so there's another five to go.'

'Oh, I *see*, then you'll move in,' Margo said enthusiastically. 'Yes, much better getting rent than having it stand empty—'

'That's exactly what I thought. And five months will be ample to put this on the market. I don't think I'll have much difficulty finding a buyer. No, I haven't quite made up my mind what I'll be doing. But time doesn't matter, and I've no restrictions on choice.'

'But . . . buyer . . . market . . .' Margo floundered.

'What will be handy, if I should move out before you find somewhere to live, you can go into the bungalow.'

After a silence, Ron croaked, 'It's only meant for one.'

'Yes, it would be a bit cramped. But you could make do, temporarily, till you'd found somewhere. Of course, I wouldn't charge you rent just for a short while.'

Another silence, then Joey asked, 'Where are you going, Granny?'

'Possibly Canada. I enjoyed the lifestyle there, I must say.'

Joey slipped out of the room, unnoticed, while Charmian said, 'But you don't like Auntie Grace.'

'You've been eating a lot of ice-cream, haven't you? I can tell by your weight.'
Charmian burst into tears.

*   *   *

Margo went furiously to Adelle. 'Where were you in all this?'
'What?'
'*What?* Letting the bungalow, what else? You were there, for Christ's sake.'
'That's true,' Adelle said, reasonable. 'But it was a *fait accompli*. The first I knew, the bungalow was finished. Someone moved in. I had no idea until that happened.'
That made sense in the dislocated lifestyles of the Saddlers. All kinds of things went on that were never mentioned and—after whatever cataclysm—never referred to.
This was different. Margo went on at length, finally shouting, 'Did you know she was going to put Longley up for sale?'
'No, not until after she'd done it,' Adelle said firmly.
'You knew bloody something. You knew something was up last time I came round. Don't think I missed that sly smirk of yours—it always means you know something.'
'What I knew was about her paying for another two weeks holiday for you. I'd promised not to say anything, not to spoil the surprise.'

'Surprise, surprise. To get me out of the way, you mean. To arrange all this with—'

'I've *told* you, I *didn't* know—'

Their voices rose, fell. When they had said what they could, Margo thumped down on the sofa. There was the silence of exhausted battle before she said, 'Is she going ga-ga?'

Adelle recovered her composure, two pink patches fading from her pale complexion. 'I'd say not.'

For once, they looked into one another's eyes. Margo said, 'Is this anything to do with . . .'

'What?'

'That night. The—accident. And then, Daddy's stroke—'

Adelle turned her gaze away, studied a cushion cover stitched with the picture of a cottage garden. Margo looked at nothing.

At last Adelle, collected, said, 'We don't know anything.'

'No, no. We don't,' Margo rushed to agree. 'It's just that the strain of it all could be, well, beginning to tell on her.'

Adelle shrugged. 'I don't know. I've never known.'

'Neither have I.'

*　　*　　*

'I told you it was useless asking Fat Ada,' Ron said later. 'She doesn't give a sod what goes on here, she's not interested.'

'She's a clever bitch,' Margo conceded.

They were in the lounge in the deepening dusk, glaring through the window at the insulting lights of the bungalow, a spurious homeliness glinting between the *cupressus leylandii*.

Margo closed the door; Violet's approach was always alerted by the thump of her stick. The children, who were not supposed to be interested in any doings except their own, had a way of materialising soundlessly on the fringes of adult conversations, or were found outside presumably closed doors unnervingly discovered ajar. As they argued, Margo kept her voice down, out of habit occasionally checking the door. 'What do you mean *move somewhere else*?' Ron said. 'What do we use for money? The old bitch never intended to move into that bungalow, she's planned this all along. *She's* been using you as a nurse maid for four years for your father and now she thinks she can shit on us. I thought you said—'

He was interrupted by the telephone. Margo barged into the hall, snatched up the receiver, snapped, 'What?'

A whispering voice said, 'Where is he? Where is he?'

'What? Who?'

'Ian. Where is he?'

Charmian appeared so abruptly she could only have been somewhere in the concealing turns and corridors of the house and not, as assumed, doing her homework in their own living room. She loomed, bulky and demanding. 'Is that for me? Lorraine said she'd ring, it's important.' As her mother was temporarily speechless, she reached out to take the receiver. Margo shoved her away, crashing the receiver to its rest. From the lounge door, Ron asked 'Who was that?'

'Dunno. Wrong number.'

Charmian said, 'Dad's promised we can have one of those new mobile phones.'

'Then let him bloody pay for it. They're the size of bricks and cost the earth.'

'Tracy's getting one for her eighteenth birth—'

'Shut up. Go away,' Margo said.

* * *

When the next call came, only Violet and Charmian were in the house.

Charmian was in her bedroom; Violet, stumping through the hall on her stick, was ideally placed to turn aside into the telephone room, take up the receiver. 'Yes?'

'Ian. He's disappeared, hasn't he? You must know.'

Violet stood absolutely still. No one was allowed to mention Ian to her, anyone who did, inadvertently and quite innocently, she dealt with impassively, staring silently at nothing, as if not a word had been said. The whispering, *slithering* voice was neither inadvertent nor innocent.

Taken completely by surprise, Violet would not give ground: she would not respond, she would not recognise, she would not hear. It took her only a moment to muster these resources, but in that time Charmian had appeared noiselessly, hovering, pressing forward, 'Is it for me? Granny, is that someone for me?'

Deliberately, Violet replaced the receiver. Her face was expressionless. 'You're not the centre of the universe.'

Charmian, accustomed to this reply, waited bovinely.

Violet said, 'Wrong number.'

'Oh, Mum got one of those the other day.'

CHAPTER NINE

When Collier went into Hunter's office on the Monday morning of a damp autumn day, Hunter gazed at him with a look in his sea-grey eyes Collier had come to recognise as the reflectiveness of inner debate.

Hunter read aloud,

'He is in love with the land that is always over

The next hill and the next, with the bird that is never
Caught, with the room beyond the looking glass.
He likes the half-hid, the half-heard, the half-lit,
The man in the fog, the road without an ending,
Stray pieces of torn words to piece together.'

Hunter was known for his mysteriously unconnected statements, outcrops of conversations carried on inside his head. The familiar, 'Hush, dears, Roger is at the pianoforte,' or 'Edna should never have touched those quern stones,' needed no response. Others posed a challenge or, worse still, demanded participation. What in God's name a poem had to do with anything at all defeated Collier. All he could manage was an interested, if inadequate, 'Er, yes.'

Hunter took pity on him and handed him a letter. Collier read,

Minim was murder. You know. You investigated. There's been another one, due to him. But no bodies asked, no bodies cared. YOU SHOULD FIND OUT. At Rush Deeping.

Its your duty.

'Is this supposed to make sense, guv?'

'Of a kind. Not grammatically, that's for sure. But I've been thinking . . . Sit down.

Listen.' A few of Hunter's troops were supremely good at that. Collier was one.

'Nineteen eighty . . . um. Eighty-five. Before your time.'

Collier was a comparative newcomer to the team. Hunter had waited for him to get his boots dirty as uniformed sergeant, then whipped him into CID after one of the old DSs retired. He had a boy's look—the shiningly clean-limbed head boy of a first rate school—was intelligent, tough and ambitious; most important, he loved his job.

Hunter explained the night of Minim's murder; the course of the investigation. Collier said, 'So we never got him?'

'No, there was never anyone in the frame. And there's never been another incident—before nor since—with any hallmarks to make a connection. We never found the murder weapon. That evening there must have been eighty, a hundred people in and out of the gallery, we never traced them all. Fingerprints everywhere, some fresh, some old. You know how it is . . .'

Collier knew. Nightmare scenario: the random, motiveless murder; the longer time passed, the less likely it would ever be solved. He looked again at the letter. 'Rush Deeping. That's that peculiar market town—towards Chester, the other side of Clerehaven. What's that got to do with it?'

'Just one of the odds and sods that never

fitted anywhere. About an hour before his death, Minim took a phone call, from a phone box in Rush Deeping. It was outside a sub-post office on a small lane that joins the A51 to Chatfield. We made a few enquiries, and the local lads kept their ears open, but we had no idea what we were looking for, who we were looking for. Could have had sod all to do with Minim's murder.'

'What about this poem, guv?'

'Another joker in the pack.' Hunter explained about the scrap of verse stuck to the back of Casement Six, noted Collier's reaction. 'You know about Fayne?'

'Well, it's not that I know anything about art, but around the time the fuss over Casements very first started, I had a friend, taught at Chatfield Art College. We used to go to galleries and exhibitions . . .'

And clubs and gay bars, and God knows where else. Not that it mattered to Hunter, and he never let it matter to anyone else in his hearing. He didn't care if anyone was male, female or both, so long as the job got done.

'. . . he was mad about Fayne's paintings, well, I didn't know they're not actually paintings, till he told me. They're drawings, aren't they? We went to Chatfield Art Gallery, to look at the one there. My friend said it was no good looking at reproductions or illustrations, you had to stand in front of a painting before you could begin to make it mean anything. He explained all about the technique and everything, but what he couldn't explain was how it generated such—weirdness . . .'

'Casement Five. The city street. Yes.'

'You've seen it?'

'Yes. I don't suppose,' Hunter asked, overcome by deja-vu, 'your friend knew who Fayne was?'

'No. He said he'd certainly never taught him, he'd have recognised the style. That was half the fascination—the mystery, and then, after the murder, there's never been another painting. Has there? I've rather lost touch with that particular—er—the art world.'

'I was never in touch. No, not as far as I know,' Hunter said. 'And *The Man in the Fog* never turned up?'

'If it has, we've never heard. Whoever's got it would have some explaining to do. Meanwhile . . .'

Collier put the letter on the desk and they both regarded it. Hunter said, 'There's nothing I can do. All right, there's an unsolved murder, and a Rush Deeping connection. Apparently. This isn't any kind of help. What the hell else this person knows, if anything, they'll have to turn up with it, we've got too much on our plate to go looking.'

Apart from this brief interlude, Hunter and his team had not a minute to spare. A critical investigation was coming to a conclusion: a local plague of upmarket burglaries. Wherever there were good class dwellings around Chatfield, with art works and antiques, there a tightly organised, professional outfit had planned and struck. It was inevitable they had come to be known as the Class Act. In every operation of that sort there was a chain: organiser, bodies on the job, drivers, receivers, fences . . . and somewhere, with luck, a police informer. As happened now. Hunter had had his tip-off, his team were keyed up, poised for observation and arrest. The last thing he was concerned with was some anonymous maunderings about an unsolved murder four and half years ago.

*   *   *

A week later, when the second letter came, WDC Annette Jones was in Hunter's office. There were still loose ends to be tidied after the successful conclusion of the Class Act, she was talking about fingerprints, how someone got careless, or overconfident, and left some that could be matched from the previous burglaries. 'It's a good result, isn't it, guv?'

Hunter, murmuring while opening his post, sat silent, reading a letter with a focused stillness that made her watch him. After a while he said, 'Another one.'

'Anonymous?'

'Mmm. Did Collier tell you?' Knowing the answer would be yes, they seemed to tell each other just about everything. They had worked so well from the word go he couldn't ask for a better team. They shared age, background, ambition, intelligence. More than that, they had the chameleon ability to make themselves acceptable almost anywhere, subduing their distinctive good looks to pass unnoticed when necessary. How Annette managed that sometimes amazed Hunter; she was tall, well built, naturally elegant, raven-haired, with a wild rose complexion. When he once expressed his surprise at the way she could transform herself undercover, she said that she didn't see what was so difficult about passing for a slag when James could pass for straight.

He handed her the letter. She read:

You've done nothing. I know, I've been watching.

He's DISAPPEARED. What's happened to him? Ask them. The Saddlers. Go on.

They looked at each other. She said, 'I'll find out.' She was soon back. 'The Saddlers, Longley House, High Martinsgate, Rush Deeping. Long established family. Straitjacket respectability. Industrial revolution money, artisans, tradesmen . . . Actually, they started out here, in Chatfield. They had a business, making luggage—'

'Of course. Saddlers, used to be in the old warehouses by the river, they're all posh apartments now. But the family must have sold out years ago.'

'Yes, the last one to be in the business died last year. He'd retired long before, though, in the sixties.'

'Where d'you get all this?'

'Sergeant Berrow at Rush Deeping; he's mad about local history, genealogy, dialects, that sort of thing. Anything you want to know about Cheshire in the last hundred years, ask Bob Berrow. You have to be ready for a quick getaway, though, or he'll bore you to death.'

'Thanks, I'll bear that in mind.'

'And odd bits I remembered.'

'Remembered?'

'Yes. Did you know the Chapel bookshop, down the hill from the old Wesleyan chapel—'

'Where the new development is. Supposed to be an improvement. Buggered if I can see it. Yes, young woman owned it. Why?'

'I didn't know her very well, but we used to chat whenever I went in. When she sold out to the developers, she decided to move to Rush Deeping, because her grandparents had lived there. Or was it her parents? Anyway, going back years, they were Saddlers. She told me about the family coming from here originally, moving to Rush Deeping in the nineteen-hundreds. So I said something about her going back amongst her own folk. She looked horrified and said no fear, the ones who live there now are ghastly. But I certainly didn't get the impression there's anything disreputable about them.'

'So why should someone try to connect them with a murder? Apart from the phone call, there's nothing—'

'Phone call?'

'The night of the murder, someone called Minim from a phone box in Rush Deeping.'

'Oh, James didn't tell me that. Still . . . hardly conclusive. Nothing you can run with, is there, guv?'

If there was, and he couldn't think what, he would have to be very cautious. It was his duty to act on information received, but anonymous letters were never given much credence—not without separate corroboration, and he couldn't see at the moment where that was coming from. If the Saddlers were in some way implicated, a premature approach would alert them, give them the chance to hide or get rid of any evidence.

'I'm going to think. I need time to pick the bones out of this,' he said.

* * *

Hunter had three busy days, then the phone call.

'You got my letters.'

A strange voice, light, yet hoarse—somebody's idea of disguise. *Spare me the drama.* 'I get a great many letters, madam.'

'How do you know I'm . . . You haven't been to Rush Deeping—'

Ah, it's you—THAT letter writer.

'You've done nothing,' accusingly.

'Perhaps you can make a suggestion.'

The ragged sound of furiously intent breathing. 'You're not taking me seriously.'

'You're not giving me any reason to.'

'Well—yes—I have. I told you—the Saddlers—' A troubled note creeping into the voice. *This young woman's not very bright, she can't even work out what she's told me and what she's imagined.* '—and about Ian disappearing.'

'Who's Ian?' Hunter asked patiently.

'Ian *Saddler*. I *said*.'

'You never mentioned a name.'

'Oh . . . I thought I had . . . I thought . . .'

'Wouldn't it be a good idea to tell me about it?'

'Well, you see, I have to be careful. If I . . . Will it be in confidence?'

Not if there's the faintest chance of it leading to the conviction of Minim's killer. 'Yes.'

'Well, I'll think about it. I'll be in touch. Don't try and trace this call, I'm in a phone box.'

*   *   *

Annette said, 'She's certainly got it in for the Saddlers. Now she says one of them's disappeared. It was murder in her first letter, wasn't it? Does she sound mad?'

'Not noticeably,' Hunter said. 'Northern

accent, not broad. She tried to disguise her voice but it kept slipping, that added to the confusion. She's going to make another approach, I know she is. At least we can try and get something in the meanwhile.' Hunter spoke thoughtfully, aware of Annette's sharpened alertness. 'That woman with the bookshop—'

'You want me to go and see her.'

'Does she know you're a detective?'

'No reason why she should. I've never mentioned what I do.'

'Right. Eggshells here. The informant could be raving or the Saddlers could be serial killers, we're working in the dark and there might not be anything at all. There's a Chatfield connection but it's so tenuous it's meaningless. Do some very gentle digging, without giving anything away. Specifically the family. This Ian—who is he? Where is he? See what you can find out. No hurry.'

'Weekend do?'

'Fine. Don't—er—don't rush to Rush.'

'That's awful, guv.'

'Take it or leave it. Best I can do at the moment.'

CHAPTER TEN

Three days later, Hunter opened his office door and grabbed the nearest person in sight: Collier. 'There's someone waiting to see me downstairs. Go and talk to her, give her a cup of tea, don't let her go.'

'Talk about what?'

'Anything. Flannel. She wants to see me about Rush Deeping.'

'The informant?'

'Must be. Where's Annette? I gave her a small job, she hasn't reported back to me yet.'

Collier was halfway down the corridor. 'I'll send her—'

Hunter had already obtained Minim's file from Records but not opened it. While he waited he sought it out, unerringly, from the mountains of paperwork on his desk. How he managed to go straight to a single item and extract it without causing a major landslide, nobody knew.

Annette came in. 'This is a turn-up.'

'If it's her, I think it must be. What did you get from the bookshop?'

'Who's who at Longley house—and I *might* just have something, though there wasn't much gossiping time. The owner, Dorcas Grey, she's seen nothing of the adults, but the young son came round, wanting to know if she had any jobs going—for cash. Apparently he's as nasty as all eleven-year-old boys, so she said no, had a bit of a job getting rid of him. Fortunately his sister came to drag him home, he was AWOL. They had a fine old set-to half in, half out of the shop, in the course of which it transpired their mother was upset because she'd had another anonymous phone call, and he said, "So what's new?" '

'Did he, by damn?'

'I pretended to be obtuse and said gosh, anonymous letters—she said no, as far as she could make out, it was phone calls.'

'Did she know what they were about?'

'No, and she couldn't be sure the kids weren't making it up. Although she said they're completely unimaginative and have never been known to make anything up before.'

'Come down with me and sit in on this. We'll have to rescue Collier, he's been talking about nothing all this time.'

Outside the interview room, Hunter told Annette to go in and send Collier out. Collier stepped into the corridor, closed the door carefully and stood looking bemused.

'Well?'

'Yes, it's her. Her name's Sandy Mathews. I gave her to understand I'm entirely in your confidence and she said she'd been getting up courage to come and see you, because it was her public duty, and she was looking forward to meeting you and . . .' He paused. 'She's, well, not what you'd, not—sort of—'

'Can you say anything sensible?'

'No, guv.'

'All right.' Hunter sighed.

He could understand Collier's reaction. Sandy Mathews, dressed in trim tracksuit and trainers, was an athletic young woman. Her crisply curling hair was cut short, her skin clear, the whites of her bright eyes the milky blue of shining health.

'Mr Hunter?' She bounced up, sat down again, limbs tomboyishly all over the place. 'You are Mr Hunter, aren't you? I know this might seem strange—well, not strange, it's all in the line of duty for you, isn't it? And, I mean, it's what you're here for, only I have to be sure I don't get into any kind of—well, put myself in—well—this has to be absolutely in confidence . . .'

He let her chatter on, sat down slowly, Annette—the target of rapid, suspicious glances—beside him. Eventually, Sandy Mathews' restlessness dwindled to a fidget, her breathy voice fell silent; she had said more or less nothing at all.

Hunter's tone was impersonal, 'Ms—er—Mathews, is it? What did you want to see me about?'

She stared. 'But . . . you know. And I just said . . .'

'No, I don't think . . . .' He turned questioningly to Annette, who shook her head.

Together, they politely regarded the young woman, who looked as if she had just cost the school its lead in the netball final.

'What? But I thought, I must have got a bit—I'm under a lot of stress.'

They smiled faintly.

'I wrote to you. I rang you up. About Ian. Saddler.'

'Yes?' Hunter said.

She sat looking miserable, temporarily wordless. 'I'm not, I can't—why don't you help?'

Annette said, 'Miss Mathew—d'you mind if I call you Sandy? Why don't you start at the beginning?'

Sandy spoke to Hunter. 'Well, you see, Ian was my friend. We've known each other since we were children.'

'And where was that?' Annette asked.

'Here, Chatfield, of course.'

'Whereabouts?'

'Chorlton Green.'

The outer urban area. Solid, small Victorian workmen's houses—enough back garden to grow vegetables, keep a few hens—mixed with aspirant thirties semis: gables, diamond leaded lights. Property once running to seed, now preserved, valued.

'And that's where you live now?' Annette asked.

Sandy said to Hunter, 'No, that's where they *sent* him, his parents, when he was *little*, to his

Auntie Catherine.'

Hunter said comfortably, 'Nice area to grow up. Nice woman—his auntie? Mrs? Miss?'

'Miss Wood. She was lovely. She died four years ago. And then Ian just—disappeared.'

'Hey, slow down a bit,' Annette said. 'Would his parents be the Saddlers at Rush Deeping?'

'Naturally.'

'So when was this—when he went to his auntie?'

Sandy cast her eyes upwards. 'I *told you*. When he was little.'

'But exactly?'

'Um. Um . . . It was . . . I was . . .' Hunter would not have been surprised if she had counted on her fingers. 'Nineteen sixty-two. Ish!

'And he lived with his auntie until her death? When was that?'

'*What*?' Sandy spared Annette a scornful glance; she plainly considered all her questions a waste of time.

'It helps to get the chronology right,' Annette said firmly. 'He lived at Chorlton Green—near you? Yes—from nineteen fifty-eight until his aunt's death—'

'Well, not exactly, not all the time . . .' She began to fidget again, muttering, looking down at her hands.

Hunter had been studying her carefully. She was not as young as she had first appeared, the boyish awkwardness and sturdy look were misleading. She was one of those people who—by the chance of nature or an act of will—remain suspended in the time, at the age they feel most secure. Without any childlike charm, she had the faintly puzzled air of a child: unable to grasp that anything should exist beyond her own wishes, that anyone else's concerns might be important.

Hunter decided, abruptly, he didn't need any of this. 'What do you do? For a living?' His change of manner was so subtle only Annette could discern it and translate: *Right, we've let her piss us about long enough.*

'I teach PE.'

Obviously. 'Where?'

'St Hilda's. Girls. It's an Independent.'

Silently, Hunter and Annette communicated bafflement. St Hilda's was so independent they'd never heard of it.

'Where's that?'

'Rush Deeping, of course.'

Annette said, 'Is that where you live?'

'Of course it's where I live. Why shouldn't I?'

She explained, somewhat defensively, that when she started at the school she had had a room there, just temporarily. Then she rented the bungalow, and it had been three months and she hadn't found out anything, although she was sure she would, being their neighbour.

Annette said, 'Whose neighbour?'

'I *told* you. The Saddlers. They'd had this

bungalow built, in the garden.' She leaned urgently towards Hunter. 'They hated him, right from being little. All of them. His father was terrible. They never wanted him, any of them. It was awful—'

Hunter said quietly, 'You are living next door to a family against whom you've made a serious allegation—'

'I haven't. I haven't alleged. I'm just saying they—'

'You send me two anonymous letters linking the name of Saddler with murder, with disappearance. You've been attempting to spy on them, and now you're making nuisance telephone calls.'

The clear skin flushed. 'I haven't, it's not me. They're not *calls*. I don't *say* anything, not now, so how can they be calls? And I had to, first, because I told you and then you didn't do anything,' she finished accusingly.

Annette said, puzzled, 'You're making nuisance calls and it's Mr Hunter's fault?'

'Well, who else? He's the only one who can get them to say why Ian's disappeared, where he is. I can't. If I came out in the open, if they found out I was Ian's friend, I could put myself in danger—'

'What has any of this to do with the murder at the Minikin Art Gallery?'

She looked at him blankly.

'*Minim was murder . . .*' he quoted her letter at her. It was obvious she had some trouble recalling it. There was no room in her small ego for interconnecting notions.

She turned her face aside as if suddenly aware of his monolithic stillness.

'Yes, well it was, wasn't it?' she said in a small voice.

'What do you know about it?'

'Well, I don't actually . . . It was one of Ian's favourite poems,' she said triumphantly. 'About the man in the fog. He often quoted it. And it was stuck on that painting with the same name, wasn't it?'

'Go on.'

'And—and he knew Minim.'

'He told you that?'

She stared into a corner of the room. 'Well, I'm not, I can't remember, not exactly—I'm getting very confused, you're not helping.'

Hunter kept his gaze on her, tapped his pen softly on the table. Annette said, 'It's not up to us to help you, Sandy. You came in here supposedly to give us information. About Minim's death. Do you mean to say the only connection you can make is that Ian liked a particular poem and he might, or just as well might not, have known Mimim?'

Sandy looked defiantly at Hunter. 'I had to make you take *notice*. It was the only way I could think to make you take notice—'

Hunter said, 'I strongly advise you to consider that if you continue your present behaviour you will be breaking the law in several ways. You are causing the police to waste time, that's an offence. Your actions against this family are verging on harassment. You've committed offences against the Telegraphy Act by making nuisance calls. If you persist in making allegations and are called on to substantiate them under oath you will be committing perjury.'

She sat completely still, her fresh complexion paling.

'As a responsible adult Ian Saddler is free to go wherever he likes, if he wishes to end his friendship with you, that's up to him. If he wishes to break his ties with his family, that's up to him. You've given us no concrete information, no reason to regard them with suspicion. You're quite right to be cautious, they could very well take legal action against you. Do you understand that?'

She said *yes* soundlessly.

'As for Ian Saddler being connected to the murder of Mr Minikin, you would do well to go home and think if you can produce a single shred of evidence. In the meanwhile I urge you very strongly to desist what you are doing.'

CHAPTER ELEVEN

With the pressure off the Class Act, its successful outcome suitably celebrated by all the troops, Hunter asked Annette and Collier to meet him one evening in the Frog and Nightgown. It actually had some recognisable, mundane name: the Waterloo Arms, the Golden Lion, but as it was one of Hunter's approved Chatfield pubs, places to revive the spirit with respectable ale and without any kind of music—then it was an official Frog and Nightgown. This might have confused some people, but Annette and Collier were learning to distinguish them by nuances: the mood he was in, their collective mood, the time of year, the weather.

'It's *Tuesday*, he *never* goes to the Stage Door on Tuesdays, it's full of old queens. Oh, sorry, James.'

'He goes to the Engineer on Friday, it's round the corner from the Reform Club and *Fridays* he has dinner at the Reform Club with all those portly old aldermen.'

'Unless he's got a date.'

'Annette, you're unhealthily obsessed with his sex life.'

'Only because I'm not part of it.'

Hunter had asked them, among other things, to look through Minim's file—'Nothing official yet, just there might be something . . .' Knowing how painstakingly they would spend their own time, because he had asked them, because they were always looking for something to take to him.

Annette told Collier about the interview

with Sandy—hard-edged, but not bullying. What Hunter had done was pull a silly creature up short, open her eyes to what she was doing, save her from harming herself or others. What Annette didn't say was that he had done it with a contained menace she hoped would never fall upon her.

He had done something else, as well. After the fall-out Annette had seen what it was. She told Collier, 'He left the door open . . . That's what he meant about a shred of evidence, if she finds anything, or remembers anything—'

'He didn't *say* it,' Collier murmured.

'No, because he's not going to encourage her nonsense, but he will listen to anything sensible. And after that she sure as hell won't take any action on her own.'

* * *

At the Frog and Nightgown they talked over what was relevant in the situation to Minim and possibly Ian. There was the poem about the man in the fog that had been stuck to the back of the painting that disappeared that night.

Annette had looked up the poet, Tessimond, discovered she'd come across one of his poems once before. 'Not this one. He's pretty obscure, fashionable at one time, nineteen thirties, so, over the years, hundreds and hundreds of people must have read his poetry.'

Hunter said, 'Obscure, yes. But we never released the quote, or any mention of it.'

Collier said, 'Minim's assistant knew about it—she told you, didn't she?'

'Yes, but I asked her to be discreet, and I'm sure she has been. Even so, any knowledge of it would have been restricted to very few people. Sandy knew it, claimed it was a favourite of Ian's and could quote it, and nobody's going to put her down as the intellectual type.'

Collier said, 'The phone call from a Rush Deeping phone box.'

'It could have been just about anyone, passing through, resident . . .'

'If that's the case, a resident would be pretty sure to have their own phone. Reasonably sure.'

'And Sandy says that Ian knew Minim. That the poem was one of Ian's favourites. That Ian's family live at Rush Deeping. That Ian has disappeared.' Collier said, adding sceptically, 'She *says*.'

Annette said, 'Guv, do you remember when Sandy said she last actually saw Ian?'

Hunter hesitated. 'I was too pissed off with the silly . . . No, Annette, I don't.'

'She was rather imprecise.'

'She was imprecise about *everything*. For what it's worth, probably nothing, we're going to leave things as they are now. Wait and see what turns up.'

*   *   *

Margo called on Adelle at Ruskin Close, taking Charmian with her. They looked first in the front window, tried the side door, pressed their faces against the reeded glass, Charmian copying her mother without question.

Margo was manhandling a black bin-liner, awkwardly shaped and tied with string. 'What's in that?' Charmian asked.

'Some stuff I'd promised Adelle for one her jumbles.'

'But you don't like Auntie Adelle.'

'Still, she's my sister.' That was unarguable and was, in Saddler terms, a sort of answer.

'But why?' Charmian persisted.

'I just hope she's in.' Margo banged the shining brass knocker.

Footsteps, a slim shape behind the obscured glass panel. Adelle expressionlessly confronted them on her doorstep.

'Hi,' Margo laughed. 'Hallo.'

There was a pause. 'I'm cold,' Charmian said.

'Yes,' Margo agreed.

Adelle stood to one side, reluctantly admitting them. Their combined, surging bulk threatened the delicate hall stand. 'I was just going to make my supper,' Adelle said.

They followed her into the kitchen. Margo

chattered while Charmian, a study in boredom, opened doors and cupboards pointlessly, watched by Adelle. 'If you've quite finished,' Adelle said, ignoring Margo.

'Have you got any computer games, Auntie?'

'You know I haven't.'

'I thought you might have got some.'

'Why on earth should I? They're for children.'

'Dad plays with ours.'

'Go in the lounge and watch TV. I want to talk to your aunt,' Margo said.

'What about?'

'This stuff I've brought her for one of her precious bring and buy sales. You'd be *very* interested.'

Charmian walked out.

Margo dropped her voice. 'I was tidying up, daren't let Mother get a sight of this, be like a red rag to a bull, especially the way she is at the moment.'

Adelle did not ask what way; she simply looked at the unwieldy package. 'The Museum Society bring and buy? What's Mother got to do with that?'

'Oh, *nothing*, that was for Charmian's benefit. Honestly, you've never had any subtlety, have you? I had to bring her along, I'm taking her to Lorraine's, some girl thing. No, I've been tidying things out. You know what's in here, overlooked in the last lot.'

Adelle said, 'Do you realise how many years ago that was?'

'I told you, I've been tidying, and I don't want her coming across . . . anything. She's just not been the same since Daddy died.'

'I haven't noticed any difference,' Adelle said, still staring at the package.

'No, well, you're not there to notice, are you? It's bound to have affected her, being alone after all those years.'

'Except she's not alone, she's got all your lot.' Adelle gave her small, cold smile. 'For the present, anyway.'

'I am getting a bit concerned.'

'You haven't settled anything yet, then?'

'What about?' Margo said impatiently.

'The bungalow—'

'Oh, that—No, it's Mother's state of mind that's worrying me.'

'What do you mean? *Oh, that.* It's all very well waving it aside but it was all you could talk about last time you were here. In fact that's *why* you were here, as I recall.'

Margo moved closer, glanced over her shoulder at the open kitchen door—an unnecessary precaution, the television was loud enough to drown even Margo's penetrating voice.

'Have you been round to Whatsit's bookshop?'

'Dorcas? No, why should I?'

'The kids have.'

'What kids?'

'Mine, for God's sake.'

'What for?' Adelle said, puzzled. 'They never read.'

'Joey's on the lookout to earn a bit of pocket money—'

'Has he started a protection racket?'

'What?' Margo stared, at a loss, shook her head. 'And Charmian goes for a snoop around. They're just being kids, but they can say some pretty daft things.'

Adelle concentrated on her supper. A fussy, fish-eating vegetarian, she prepared salad, beans, Quorn and tofu.

Margo said, 'I don't know how you can eat that junk.' Her family dined robustly on burgers, pizzas, take-away Chinese, battered fish and chips. They all struggled with their weight, except Joey, who had inherited the errant gene that streamlined Adelle.

'I hear she's bought a house at Mechanics Yard. You know, those conversions. I understand they're really special, very sympathetic modernisation.' Margo said nothing, went to the kitchen door and stared towards the noise issuing from the lounge. Adelle continued, 'So, talking about somewhere to live. You haven't arranged anything—'

'Who said that?'

'You did, just now.'

'No, I didn't. Your trouble is you never

listen, you're only concerned about yourself, never anyone else. Everything's settled, Mother's just being awkward. But she's in such a funny state.' Margo returned to stand beside Adelle at the worktop, leaned forward confidingly. 'Daddy's death, that fall she had in Canada. And we know how difficult it's always been since . . . that night . . . the accident, when Daddy had his stroke. We've never really understood . . .'

'Speak for yourself,' Adelle said, busy with knife, chopping board, herbs.

'What do you mean? I *told* you.'

'I've never made any sense of what you told me, except that you'd sorted it all out with Mother.'

'Yes, well . . .'

Margo looked out of the kitchen window, Adelle stared down at her preparations. It was not a conspiracy, it was the Saddler habit of not seeing, not knowing, not saying.

'But what with one thing and another . . .' With her foot Margo nudged the bundle she had dumped in a corner of the kitchen. 'It would just be so unsettling for her to be reminded of, well, anything, so we daren't let her see anything . . . that . . . You know.'

'Daren't let Granny see what?' Charmian said from the open kitchen door.

CHAPTER TWELVE

On the outskirts of Rush Deeping, Hunter slowed as he passed the noticeboard 'St Hilda's Independent Day School for Girls 4 to 18 years'. Aristocratic wrought iron gates, a distant large house clad in scarlet Virginia creeper. There was no one in sight on the sweeping playing fields, no doubt mad Ms Mathew was bouncing about a superbly fitted gym with lots of well bred little girls. He had a wicked impulse to call in and shock her back into her senses. Realistically, he knew he had pretty well done that as far as it was possible, and from what he knew of expensive private schools, mild eccentricity was the norm.

He slowed again along quiet High Martinsgate, caught glimpses of Longley House behind its concealing conifers and overgrown shrubs. The bungalow was clearly in view down the side driveway, raw-looking in the graceful road, barricaded by its builders' rubble. Even when that had been cleared and a garden laid out, it would still be ugly.

He followed his nose around Rush Deeping. It was not a place he had ever, professionally or socially, had occasion to visit. What he saw was an old market town in the act of turning its back on the past: conversions, gentrifications; oases of modern houses, aggressively rustic, crowded together on lost gardens and orchards. It had its fair share of the intricate black and white buildings that had been standing around in the towns of Cheshire for three hundred years, but the market square had given way to rampant commercialism, olde tea shoppes and takeaways; a bookmakers (people in Rush Deeping had money to chuck about). Beeching had done away with the railway link to Chatfield, the Victorian Gothic station was a garden centre, the Workhouse an Italian restaurant.

At Rush Deeping police station he paid his courtesy call on Inspector Rodney Armstrong, an ambitious young man, new to the town, who looked on his job as a developmental move, carrying more responsibility than an ordinary shift Inspector. Rush Deeping was a stepping stone; Hunter had the impression of being caught between one stride and the next as Rodney Armstrong propelled himself towards his future. He knew the feeling.

When Hunter asked about the Saddlers, Armstrong said with helpful incomprehension, 'The Saddlers?' They had no record of wrong-doing, of anything; as far he was concerned, there was no reason he should know about them.

'It's a funny situation,' Hunter said, explained briefly about Sandy Mathew, her friendship with Ian Saddler, her conviction—delusion—that his disappearance was suspicious.

'As far as I know we've never had anything on the family. I can check if you like, sir.'

'They haven't come to you recently with any complaint about being harassed?'

Armstrong shook his head.

'Nuisance calls?'

'Definitely not. That I'd know about.'

'They've been established here for a long time. The old man died last year but his son wasn't at the funeral,' Hunter pressed.

'There could be any number of reasons for that.'

'Yes. More or less what we think. It could be something or nothing. I'd just like to check with your sergeant, though. I understand he knows everything that's happened round here for the last hundred years.'

'Doesn't he bloody just. Try and stop him,' Armstrong said feelingly.

Bob Berrow, a placid countryman nearing retirement, was too proud of his local knowledge to allow it to be downgraded, even by a DCI. 'History is my thing,' he informed Hunter sententiously. 'Modern families, that'd be gossip, sir, I don't do that.'

But he plainly did and Hunter left, replete with it, half an hour later.

*   *   *

Whatever Margo wanted in the shop had nothing to do with books. She went straight up to Dorcas, who was chatting with a customer. 'I don't suppose you've seen Mother.'

'Mother?'

'My mother. Your—er—aunt.'

'Is she?'

'Well, something of the sort. Relative. Don't ask me. Have you seen her?'

'About what?'

'Well, I thought she might take it into her head, you know.' Margo's loud voice, then her laugh, crashed into quiet corners.

'No,' Dorcas said, baffled.

The customer began a polite retreat, 'Look, if this is a family matter, I can look after myself and let you two—'

'Not at all,' Dorcas said firmly. 'Here—this is our folklore section. We have—oh, yes, here—*Ritual to Romance*, which I think is the sort of thing you're—'

Margo elbowed her way between them. 'Look, won't have to wait long. I'm really pushed for time.' To Dorcas, 'I've got to collect Charmian from her trumpet lesson.'

With the notion of torpid and overweight Charmian blowing a trumpet an air of bedlam threatened to take over the shop.

The customer said, 'I'm really not in any—'

'Good. Where can we talk—oh, there'll do.' Margo hauled Dorcas behind the counter.

Dorcas protested, 'Margo, I can't just—'

'This is something you ought to know, as family. Mother's never been the same since

Daddy died.'

'Oh, hasn't she? I didn't—'

'No, well. I had *hoped*, you know. Now we could all *settle* down and after all the devoted care and support I've had to give, well, there'd be space for me, myself. Pick up my career where I left off to devote myself to the family, then Daddy. I was going into social work, because I'm so good with people.'

'Are you?' Dorcas questioned faintly.

'But now, it seems Mother's going to be a problem. She's started wandering off.'

'I'm sorry to hear that, but—she can't get far, surely. Didn't she have an accident while she was away? And has to walk with a stick?'

'Don't you believe it, she can cover a surprising amount of ground. And now she's imagining all sorts of people are phoning her up.'

'Phoning *her*? But, I thought it was you who . . .'

'Me what?

'Well, receiving anonymous calls. Your children were in here, they said—'

'Don't take any notice of the kids, they get everything wrong.' Being Margo, she repeated everything twice, unstoppably, finishing, 'Listen, Mother *might* take it into her head to wander in here. If she does, just politely offer her a lift and take her home, but don't make it obvious.'

'My assistant isn't always here, I can't just

leave the shop if I'm on my own, with customers here—'

'No one comes in much, do they?' Margo looked at the one customer. 'Not that I can see.'

'I do have busy times—'

'What? If you say so. And I suppose it's too much to expect you to put yourself out for us. Just give me a ring. It's no good phoning Fat Ada, even if she's at home she's always too taken up with her own concerns to give a damn about Mother. Now, don't go talking about this all over the place. It calls for tact. I mean, it's embarrassing; sort of thing that's best kept in the family. And Mother would be furious at the mere suggestion she was going a bit ga-ga.'

Margo surged out, leaving Dorcas with the stranded thought: *Who the bloody hell's Fat Ada?*

CHAPTER THIRTEEN

Detective Chief Superintendent Garret's office at Headquarters. Hunter said, 'That's it, sir, that's as far as I've got, and all I've got.'

After some thought, Garret spoke. 'Bit problematical, wouldn't you say Sheldon? You've got a family so respectable they haven't had so much as a parking ticket between them. A rational adult who has every right to take himself off from a mad girl. I know I would, in his shoes. And said mad girl's been sending you anonymous letters and making nuisance calls to the family. You think.'

'She admitted it.'

'She sounds to me the type who'd admit anything, so long as any bugger listened.'

'Yes, there's that.'

'And there's been no complaint from the family.'

Hunter shook his head, he'd explained his recce at the local nick had turned up nothing at all. There was no point in reading too much into the fact that the family had never reported the calls, they needn't necessarily wish to conceal them—fat chance with the two Saddler children talking all over the place. They had possibly regarded them as no more than a minor nuisance that would go away in time. As it had.

All Hunter had got, as he admitted to Garret, was shreds and patches, but the fact that he was bothering at all meant that he sensed something. And Garret knew that. It had never ceased to rankle with him that Minim's murder had been in the records so many years as 'unsolved'. At the time it occurred it had been sensational and then . . . slipping from headlines, attention, interest. And yet, this violent act still needed its solution—for the sake of the victim, his grieving friends, society.

'I've always said we'll get the bastard one day.'

'Yes.' Hunter provided the grace notes. 'You have.'

Decisively, 'OK. I've got a bit of money in the overtime budget . . . What about manpower?'

'I have my own ideas.'

'No doubt,' Garret said dryly. 'Play it your way, Sheldon. I don't know why I bothered to say that, you always do.'

* * *

Back at his office, Hunter found a message from Annette, who had gone off duty. *Mad Sandy wanted to speak to you. SHE'S REMEMBERED SOMETHING.*

And what that said, between the lines, was that Sandy wasn't going to tell Annette, she wasn't going to tell anyone except Hunter.

He smiled. Annette, elegant, subtle, dedicated, could charm responses from all kinds of unlikely people, but she was clever enough to know when not to waste effort. His thoughts turned to WPC Mary Clegg, who had been in his mind when he spoke to Garret. Mary could not be more of a contrast. With her, subtlety was unknown. She was conscientious, dogged, sensible as a thermal vest—although she had recently surprised him by demonstrating a wonderful gift for mimicry.

When he called her into his office she presented herself smart and stocky, her plain, unmade-up face always ready with a smile, her straight hair tied back in a ribbon.

'Mary, just for now, this is on the Q.T. I've got a job on that's just a bit iffy, I need different skills, different inputs. I haven't spoken to your shift inspector yet, but I'd like you in on it—'

'Yes, sir,' she said before he'd finished speaking.

'Hang on, you don't know what it is.'

She would never say anything as reckless as *I don't care* but her face said it for her. 'No, sir.'

'It's a plain clothes job, but as it'll only be bits here and there I don't suppose I'll be able to get you an allowance, so if you . . .'

'That's all right, sir, there's nothing much to spoil. I've never been what you could call a fashion statement.'

That was true, neat and serviceable just about summed Mary up.

'Right. What it is, there's just the possibility of something turning up in connection with a unsolved murder in nineteen eighty-four, the Minikin—'

'Art Gallery. Minim,' she said promptly, adding, visibly awed, 'That would be something.'

'And it might be absolutely nothing,' he said warningly. She had the same runaway look he'd seen so often in Annette and Collier and she was supposed to be the drogue on their hurtling enthusiasms. 'There's a contact, of a kind, in Rush Deeping. I want you to come out there with me—about an hour, OK? Then I can let you know what's going on—as much as there is. But not a word to anyone, till I've seen your boss. Right.'

* * *

Dusk gathered as they drove to Rush Deeping. Hunter, impressed by her recollection of Minim's murder, found he didn't need to go over any ground there. He told her about Sandy, her letters, phone calls, her obsession with Ian Saddler's disappearance.

'Has he?' Mary asked.

'He was never much in evidence, not at Rush Deeping, not according to Sandy and Bob Berrow—he's the local sergeant with a nose like an anteater for gossip. Ian's mother farmed him out to an aunt at Chatfield when he was five or six, she had some sort of illness or something, couldn't cope with a small child and two older daughters. From time to time he went back home as he grew up, but he could never get on with his father. The father, Joseph, died last year, by all accounts an old sod. The son never attended the funeral, hasn't put in an appearance since. Joseph had had a series of strokes, that's why the youngest daughter, Margo, lives with her mother, she helped nurse him. She's married to a chap who owned a garage locally, he's got a history of sharp trading and shady deals, but he's never fallen foul of us. Not yet, anyway. None of them have.'

'They don't seem like the kind of folk who'd have much do with Minim.'

'Right. It could all be in Sandy's imagination.' He told her about *The Man in the Fog*, then about Sandy renting the bungalow, making the nuisance calls.

After thought, Mary said, 'A bit bonkers.'

'Well, she certainly doesn't go in for joined-up thinking.'

Darkness had fallen by the time they drove through the dense belt of trees that guarded Rush Deeping, into the outer residential area. For people accustomed to the city, it was a strangely towering darkness, with the lights of quiet old houses beyond long gardens; tall sentinel trees, half stripped for winter, keeping watch along empty roads, the magnificent ghostliness of a barn owl swooping for a moment in their headlights.

Hunter drove along the wide drive of Longley House, past the opening on the left where it continued, curved, plunged between the leylandiis towards the out of sight house. He pulled in beside the bungalow. Sandy must have heard his car, footsteps, seen him through the spy-hole as soon as he rang the bell. She wrenched open the door, thrust her hands forward as if to grab him, haul him in. 'What are you doing here . . . what if they see . . . I only wanted to . . . supposing they *see*—WHO'S THAT?'

He halted the torrent of words calmly, 'Sandy, it's dark, no one can see us from the house. This is WPC Mary Clegg.'

'What if there's someone in their garden, and they *see*—'

'I doubt there will be in the dark, love,' Mary said, always practical. 'And if anyone does ask you can tell them your aunt and uncle came to visit you.'

Such a mundane notion would never have occurred to Sandy; she grasped it as a life-line, regarded Mary with grudging respect, showed them quickly in through a tiny hall, into a large living room. She stood there, silent, regarding Hunter.

'You left a message,' he prompted.

'What? Oh, well, you said if anything . . . when you asked how I knew Ian knew Minim. But you'd got me all flustered, you and that other detective and I couldn't think straight and . . .'

He let her talk herself down. When she came to a stop the silence suggested she had achieved something.

He sighed inwardly. 'So what is it you've remembered?'

'Well, I *said*. It was my stepfather.'

'You didn't, and what has he got to do with it?'

'He knew Minim, he was always going in art galleries and studios.'

'He's an artist, your stepfather?'

'No,' she said, bewildered why it wasn't perfectly clear to him. 'No, of course he wasn't. He was the art critic on the *Chatfield Argus*.'

A scarcely measurable pause. 'Your stepfather was Archie Barnes?'

'Yes. You knew him, you knew he wasn't an *artist*.' She gave an explosive giggle at the idiocy of the idea. 'That was why I knew you'd want to know about Ian, and everything. Archie always said you were,' she floundered, cast about. 'Human? Humane? Humanit—?'

'You knew a quote from one of Ian's favourite poems was stuck on the back of the painting that went missing—Casement Six,' Hunter said with weary exactitude. 'How did you know?' He waited, gave her time; he wasn't going to put ideas in her head, not that there was much likelihood they would stay there long.

Eventually she murmured uncertainly, 'Archie . . . ?'

'That'll do. Mary, go and make us a cup of tea.'

'I've only got herbal,' Sandy said.

'Anything'll do.' Mary went out, leaving the door open. As they spoke they could hear her clinking about the kitchen, got occasional glimpses as she moved to and fro.

Hunter sat down, talked about Archie, who had died shortly after retirement. She was too self-absorbed to think about the effect of anything she said until after she had said it; if he stampeded her she would become confused and cease to make any kind of sense at all. She had been fond of Archie, 'Such a lovely, funny man. So understanding. He took me to the theatre with him sometimes and art galleries, he loved paintings. Later on, when we were older, Ian sometimes came with us.'

'And did you go with him to Minim's?' Hunter asked carefully.

'No, I never went there, obviously I'd have remembered, wouldn't I? Archie took Ian. It was when I was at college in Bradford.'

'Archie was at Minim's the night he was murdered. Did he talk to you about it?'

'Well, he was upset, because they'd been friends. But I never knew Minim, so it didn't mean anything.'

'No, it wouldn't,' Hunter agreed, with unrecognised irony. 'Can you think of anything he said about that night—who was there, who he spoke to?'

She said no, restively, her interest wandering.

He waited in silence until her attention returned to him. 'Was Ian with your father that night?'

She blinked. 'No. Well, he never *said*, and

Archie didn't.' It was plainly a thought that was new to her.

'Surely Ian would have told you, when he talked to you afterwards about it.'

'I was away at college.'

As she regarded that as a complete answer, Hunter tried from a different direction. 'So Ian was interested in art. Did he paint?'

'*Paint*?' She struggled with the idea. 'How d'you mean?'

'Paint pictures,' Hunter said slowly.

'Pictures?'

'Never mind.'

'He wasn't much into sport,' she volunteered.

It took time and rapidly deteriorating patience, but eventually Hunter got there. She had not seen Ian at all since the murder. He had telephoned her occasionally and once or twice written to her.

Through the open kitchen door he could see Mary hovering; he gave the slightest nod. She came in, managing three mugs of something that smelled like a compost heap on a hot day. Nothing would induce Hunter to drink it.

'Written—then you have an address.'

'What?'

Mary said, 'As your boyfriend he'd want you to keep in touch.'

The unguarded pleasure on Sandy's face told Hunter that to have Ian acknowledged as her boyfriend was a kind of triumph for her—even though he had left her and, if in his right mind, would stay resolutely unfound. 'Yes, I suppose so.'

There was a short silence. Mary said patiently, 'If you could let us have a look at his letters—just to check the address, that's all.'

'Oh, I haven't got them any more,' Sandy said as if it was something everyone was expected to know.

'What?' Hunter breathed.

She explained that when he first wrote he said his address was only temporary; after a while he wrote again but gave no address. She had herself moved twice since then and in one of the moves the bundle of letters had disappeared.

'Can you remember the address?' Mary asked. That was rather too much. Sandy screwed up her face in an effort of memory. Brighton. Sebastian something—House? Hall?

Hunter asked her if she'd had any contact with the family since he last spoke to her.

She looked puzzled. 'What sort of contact?'

'Contact as in making anonymous telephone calls,' he said stonily.

'No, I haven't.' She was strenuously indignant, as if the notion was outrageous.

Eventually, she got round to telling him that the day the family came back from holiday the boy, Joey, came and knocked on her door. But she hadn't *asked* him, she hadn't *expected* him, she hadn't done anything Hunter told her not to do.

'Of course not,' Mary agreed. 'He came round here of his own accord, you didn't invite him, did you? No. What did he want, love?'

'I dunno. Just curious, I think. He said he'd do jobs if I paid him.'

'Did you?' Hunter asked.

'What could he do?' she said, looking round helplessly.

There was the minimum of furniture, plain and practical, cheap rugs on bare boards, unmatched throws over chairs, no lampshades, sports equipment littered everywhere. The living room was fitted with a large gas fire of overpowering ugliness. The air had the faintly breathing chill of not yet dried plaster; the walls were emulsioned a flat blue, the yellow curtains were much too long and crumpled up on to the narrow window ledges. She obviously had no home-making instinct but then, this wasn't her home, it was somewhere she had paused in her pursuit of her "boyfriend".

Hunter said, 'You've been trying to get at the family since you came here, that's *why* you're here. Don't tell me you didn't pump him for information when you had the chance.'

'I didn't, I didn't—' There were protestations, breathless narratives weaving here and there; the eventual sense he made of it was that young Joey had told her something about there being a big row because his grandmother was going to go and live in Canada and this seemed to upset everyone. 'But he wouldn't know anything, anyway, he's only a kid. I don't think he's very bright.'

From what he had heard of the opportunistic way Joey turned up wherever he thought there was money to be earned, Hunter could scarcely resist thinking, *He's a bloody sight brighter than you.*

CHAPTER FOURTEEN

Two days later Hunter received a phone call from Rodney Armstrong at Rush Deeping to tell him that Mrs Violet Saddler had been reported missing. 'In view of your interest, I thought you'd better know.'

Hunter said, 'How missing?'

'This is as far as it goes. Her daughter, Mrs Margo Duggan, came in two hours ago to report her mother's not in the house this morning, her bed hasn't been slept in, and there's no sign of her anywhere. She last saw her late yesterday afternoon when she drove her to the Market Square, left her there to make her own way to spend the evening with her other daughter, Mrs Adelle Kenning, lives in Ruskin Close.'

Hunter's first thought was of Sandy. He would say he had frightened her enough to stay in the background, but her inability to consider anything beyond herself and her obsession about Ian made her an uncomfortable lurking presence.

'You've done a thorough search of her home address?'

'Yep, it's a big house, garden, there are outbuildings. We've been through everything.' Armstrong stampeded into impressive detail. Hunter understood his ambition—but why did he have to be such an objectionable sod while he was about it?

'And the bungalow?'

'Right, sir. I remembered about that, the dippy tenant. She's not there, it's half term, she left at the weekend to stay with her mother, but we got in, the daughter had a spare key. We gave it a good going over, nothing. We've done all the checks, neighbours, relatives, likely places. The daughter's tried everywhere. Says her mother could be confused; she had an accident last year and lately she's taken to wandering off.'

'Then why leave her in the market square? Why not drive her to this other daughter?'

'Old girl wanted to do a bit of shopping. She walked with a stick but she was fit enough, believed in exercise, often walked up to Ruskin. Stubborn as hell, apparently.'

'What about this other daughter? What does she have to say?'

'Nothing, yet. She's at work and not

contactable.'

'Why?'

'That's according to Mrs Duggan—she's in a bit of a state, and not making much sense. Inclined to be a bit hysterical. She just says you can never get through to her sister, she's left an urgent message to phone but she says she never responds to messages. She works at Government House. Department of Environment.'

'That's here, on the bypass.'

'Yep. That's why we haven't done anything yet. Thought—it's on the doorstep for you and—'

'Yes. Worth paying her a visit. Right. Leave that with me, I'll get back to you when we've seen her. Meanwhile, anything turns up, let me know.' As yet he had no justification for diverting specialist resources, but he needed to know the state of play. The sister, who by account was the last person to see old Mrs Saddler, was virtually within walking distance and Annette and Collier were already aware of the situation . . .

*　　*　　*

Annette and Collier were shown into an office colourless, impersonal and ferociously ordered. When they had introduced themselves Adelle said, 'Well?' with a stare guaranteed to keep everyone at a distance.

'Your mother is Mrs Violet Saddler of Longley House, Rush Deeping?' Annette asked.

'Yes.'

'Did you drive her home last night?'

Adelle raised fine eyebrows. 'Why should I?'

'She had supper with you.'

'First I've heard of it.'

Collier said, 'You mean you never saw your mother last night?'

'No, I've told you,' brusquely. 'What is all this about?'

'So you weren't at home last night?' Annette said.

On Adelle's pale-skinned, expressionless face the cheekbones coloured the faintest pink. 'Where I was is entirely my own business.'

'I just meant that if your mother had—'

'Nothing's happened to her, has it?'

'We hope not, Mrs Kenning, but it would seem that she's missing,' Annette said gently.

Adelle struggled visibly with disbelief before saying weakly, 'But that's silly, Mother couldn't be *missing*. What do you mean?'

Collier began to explain about her sister going into Rush Deeping police station. She interrupted him crisply, 'If Margo's in this it's bound to be nonsense, she's dramatising something out of all proportion. She's always doing it.'

'You're telling us not to take this seriously?'

That made her pause. 'No. Well, I . . .' Her slim hands spread. 'You don't mean she's been missing since yesterday? All night?'

Annette explained how her sister had assumed Mrs Saddler had returned late but in the morning found her bed had not been slept in.

'My mother is tidy and disciplined, she always makes her own bed. And if she'd decided to get up and go out early this morning, there's no earthly reason why she shouldn't. I think you'll find there's some entirely reasonable explanation and Margo is just being hysterical.'

Collier asked that, if that was the case, could she suggest where her mother might have gone.

She thought for a moment, produced a handbag from somewhere out of sight and drew a diary from it. 'The Gables, a private hotel just outside Knutsford, it belongs to relatives of ours. There's a family do on, an eighteenth birthday party. For all the youngsters . . . I couldn't think that Mother might go but I suppose it's just possible.'

Collier said, 'Wouldn't your sister have thought of that?'

'Don't ask me what Margo thinks. I doubt she ever does.'

'If you'd let me have the telephone number we can call from here and check.'

With a cold, patronising smile, Adelle said, 'This is nothing to do with outsiders. I really can't have you telephoning—'

Annette, brisk, polite, said, 'Mrs Kenning, we're here on an official enquiry, we don't have time to waste. Your co-operation will assist us in clearing up the matter of your mother's whereabouts.'

In an arctic silence Adelle looked up the number and gave it to Annette, who thanked her politely. Her call was answered immediately but it took several moments of shouting against a background of ear-splitting music, before she prized an answer out of one of several dangerously stupid teenagers—a performance watched expressionlessly by Adelle.

She put the receiver down. 'No, as you thought, Mrs Kenning, your mother's not—'

'Of course she isn't, it was scarcely worth the effort.'

'We wouldn't be doing our job properly if we didn't—'

Adelle waved this aside, abruptly displayed a momentary glacial anger. 'It's too bad. I can't think what Margo's playing at. She should have told me Mother's missing before she made this official. She knows where I am, for goodness' sake, she could have picked up the phone.'

In defence of an unknown and obviously detested Margo, Annette said, 'I understand she left an urgent message for you to phone her, and she seems to have difficulty contacting you—'

'Nonsense. I can't remember the last time she tried, but that's nonsense anyway. As for a message—' She picked up the phone, made some decisive queries. It did not take long, she was not the kind of woman to waste time on small talk or explanations. 'I thought not,' she said eventually. 'None of my staff would neglect to pass on a message.'

They wouldn't *dare*. Collier said, 'Your sister seems to think your mother has become absent-minded.'

'She's as sharp as a needle, she always has been.' Her voice lost its crispness, there was suddenly a suggestion of something unsettled.

They waited silently, studying her, resolutely courteous, giving her nowhere to go.

'Well, just recently she did say she was concerned. But I thought it was just Margo exaggerating . . .'

'Were you at home yesterday evening?'

'Wednesdays I go to a craft club.'

'So your mother might have gone round, while you were out.'

'She *never* just drops in, she always phones first.' Again, a hesitation in the positive voice.

Annette said, 'If you can have a word with your neighbours, in case anyone saw her.'

'Yes, yes, that would be sensible. And now, if there's nothing else, I'll have to finish early and go and see what Margo thinks she's up to.' She rose, briskly set them in motion towards the door, 'So if you'll excuse me, I'm extremely busy.'

They murmured they would see themselves out. Before closing the door Annette glanced back. Adelle had taken her seat again behind her meticulous desk, staring straight ahead, for an instant there was expression on her face: bewilderment, a glancing fear.

* * *

Collier said, 'I think it'll turn out to be domestic cross purposes, guv. Mrs Kenning's inclined to dismiss the whole thing. She's a . . .' He paused.

'High-handed bitch,' Annette supplied. 'She really didn't believe her mother could be missing, inclined to shrug the whole thing off as some drama made up by the other sister.'

'Anything else?'

Collier looked at Annette, when she nodded, he said, 'It probably isn't anything, but she resented us asking where she was last night. We both felt she wasn't telling the truth.'

'We can't be sure. It's just, I'd say she was one hundred per cent honest about everything else. Especially her opinion of her sister,' Annette said wonderingly. 'Sibling rivalry I know. That was something awesome. And we could be wrong . . .'

Hunter considered. 'Let Rodney Armstrong know how it went, then unless something else comes up, we'll leave it to the local lads, it's their misper. The old lady's probably perfectly safe somewhere and just forgotten to tell anyone.'

CHAPTER FIFTEEN

Hunter spoke to Mary Clegg's shift inspector and in due course Mary presented herself, a picture of restrained eagerness.

'Mary, I've got a small job for you.'

'Same enquiry, sir? Rush Deeping?'

'Yes. Old Mrs Saddler's gone missing, since last night, it seems. One daughter reported her missing, the other one thinks it's a fuss about nothing.' He explained the position, said, 'I've had a thought. I want you to put your visiting hat on—'

The eagerness faded: was this one of the famous non-sequiturs that were known to induce panic in the fainthearted?

'You remember Sandy's mother lives at Chorlton Green. Here's the address.'

'You want me to call round?' Mary said with relief. 'But—do you think Sandy could have anything to do with the old lady going missing?'

'No, she's been staying with her mother

since the weekend—I need to make sure of that. And find out if she knows anything she doesn't know, if you follow me. Tell her you've come to apologise for going in to the bungalow in her absence, play it concerned—you know the drill. Better still if her mother's there, you might get some sense. Keep your eyes and ears open.'

When Mary reported back Hunter was in the CID office, sitting round and—in Annette's case—on Collier's desk. There were ten people around hard at work, some listening with the backs of their heads, others too pushed to take any notice of anyone. Registering that DC Terence Bale was sitting at the next desk, Hunter took a bet with himself how long it would be before there was some extra input. 'OK, Mary, tell it how it was.'

Sandy's mother was alone when Mary called, not that it mattered; with assurances that Sandy would be back in no time, she had Mary settled before the fire with a cup of tea and a slice of lemon sponge. There was an interlude that could only be described as comfy, Mrs Barnes being a kind, rather vague woman, stockful of gossip, confidences, reminiscences.

Ian, such a nice boy, always quiet and well-mannered. It was tragic, the way his family treated him, *his mother didn't want him.* Could there be anything so unnatural? But there you are, these things happen. Fortunately, there was Auntie Catherine, a nicer woman you couldn't wish to meet. Dead now, poor love. She gave him all the care he needed. And, of course, being just round the corner, he and Sandy grew up together, inseparable as kiddies.

Childhood sweethearts? Mary asked, with, Hunter had no doubt, just the right amount of sentimental understanding. He was beginning to appreciate there was more subtlety to her than he had imagined.

Well, Mrs Barnes didn't know about that. Sandy had never been one for boyfriends, not romance and things like that. As for Ian he was, well, just a nice youngster, always so helpful, wonderful choosing colours, for curtains and things, he even did the flower arranging . . .

('Did he make his own frocks?' Annette breathed. Hunter growled, 'If I'd said that you'd be shouting 'sexism' and—' 'Yes, all right, sorry, guv.')

. . . and he kept trying, with his family, going to see them, keeping in touch, and then he'd come back, hurt and upset. They weren't nice people, they weren't at all nice.

Aware of time passing, of Sandy's imminent return, Mary asked about Ian's disappearance—to be blandly assured that he just went off, always a loner. Perhaps that was why he and Sandy hit it off so well, she was quite a bit of a loner herself, and (off on another tack) Archie had always been so good with her, endless patience. She'd never have got into University without him—she'd always been wonderful at sport, but never academic, you know. Kept on failing exams. Late starter, Archie said, and he gave her so much help, coaching her. Mary, following Hunter's instructions, seized on an opening, 'He was good at that, wasn't he? He encouraged Ian's interest in art, didn't he?'

'Did he?'

'So Sandy told me. He used to take him to Minim's—you remember, that gallery owner who was murdered. Archie was there that night, terrible business. Did he speak to you about it?' Mary, with her gift for mimicry, switching between her own voice and what was undoubtedly Mrs Barnes's, held them spellbound.

'Oh, he didn't bring nasty things home with him. He never liked upsetting anyone, didn't Archie.'

'Did he ever say to you that Ian was with him that night?'

Here, all Mary's professionalism foundered on Mrs Barnes' blank stare.

Returning comfortably to Ian, Mrs Barnes said he would probably turn up again, it was what he was always doing. You never knew when he'd just take himself off. Mary said, 'Sir, I don't think Ian, his disappearance, Minim's murder, had any significance in her life at all.

If it had in Archie's . . .' she shrugged.

'He must have kept it to himself,' Annette supplied.

'Yes.' And it had been at that point, before she could find another opening, that Sandy returned. Hunter asked how she had reacted to finding Mary there.

'Fine. Pleased, in fact, her mother loves company. A bit furtive, I realised that was because she wouldn't want her mother to know about the anonymous letters and phone calls, but I think she trusted me not to get her into bother with her mum.'

Mary told her about Mrs Saddler, and the bungalow being searched. Sandy took Mrs Saddler's disappearance if not with concern—in the small ego of Sandy's world there was no room for concern for anyone except herself—at least with surprise. Her mother had gone off to make fresh tea, and she was anxious to assure Mary the old lady's disappearance had nothing to do with her. She was relieved they had been in the bungalow, because it proved she had nothing to hide.

Mary said she didn't doubt it, and if she could just help them out by remembering anything Archie had said about Ian being at Minim's private view. Sandy had been too confounded by the change of subject to say anything sensible—('Now there's a surprise,' Annette murmured.)—so even if he did tell her anything it obviously never registered, and she'd certainly forgotten. Like mother, like daughter.

DC Terence Bale, bursting with the effort of pretending to get on with his work, gave up and turned his chair round. 'Guy, I knew Archie, I was there that night . . .'

Yes, of course you were, you were still in uniform, and along with all the others doing what was necessary: taking statements, questioning everyone present, asking about other people there: Who did you recognise? Who could you name? And later, collating statements . . .

'I took his statement. He gave the names of a lot of people he knew, but he never mentioned an Ian Saddler . . .'

The police passion for knowing and talking—like to like—ensured an underground ferment of gossip. Terence Bale had only to catch the faintest suggestion of a possible review of an investigation he had once been involved in (and he could not have failed to pick up the signals Annette and Collier had been giving out)—he would have found it easier to choke than keep quiet.

Bale said, 'This artist, the whole shindig was for him but he was supposed not have turned up.'

Hunter said, 'Supposed?'

'Thing is, there was some talk he was there—'

'Whose talk?'

'That's just it, guv, I can't remember. It was all a bit inconclusive . . . someone's bound to know what exactly was said—or hinted.'

Bale was reliable but hamhanded, hints had to be stone cladded to mean anything to him; if somewhere in that gaudy, precious crowd there had been nuances, insinuations, he would have blundered right through them in his size tens without noticing.

Collier said, 'There was a heck of a crowd.'

Annette said, 'Did Archie stay to the end?'

'Possibly not, he was famous for leaving when he'd had enough. You mean, Fayne might have turned up later.'

Mary said, 'What about security cameras in the area? What do they tell us about coming and goings.'

Bale said, 'We're not talking about an area. We're talking about one of Chatfield's many arseholes. No one sticks security cameras up them, even now.'

Hunter said, 'I couldn't have put it better myself.'

* * *

Early the following morning, a young couple jogged along the path beside Merlin Mere, enthusiastically accompanied by their black retriever.

The previous day had been unrelieved, pelting rain, now a red gold sun was rising, the trees burning russet in its light. A frail mist masked distances, curled from hollows, crept across the surface of the water.

Merlin Edge loomed above the mere, an escarpment of red sandstone riddled with ancient, abandoned copper mines. At one point a sheer drop, the rest a wavering length of paths and clearings, heavy with birch, oak, pine, tangled with bushes, haunted by wildlife, lovers, ghosts. Legend had it a wizard lived in one of the caves. If you discovered his cave you could foretell the future.

The highest point of the Edge was famous for its view of two counties meeting: a rolling landscape of woods and farms, rich pastures, contained market towns, spires, great houses; here, since recorded time, a beacon had signalled great events.

The couple splashed through puddles, through the glory of the morning, its pure and fragile air. To their left a rough space of dying grasses covered with spiders' webs that shimmered in soft grey veils of minute droplets.

To their right the mere and rising from it the toppling threat of the precipice.

We won't go up today, there isn't time—

No, halfway, then we'll cut for home—

The retriever, left behind, tearingly overtook them, plunged into the mere, sending up plumes of water in his ecstatic flounderings.

They passed, after a while called back,

Come on, come on, old boy. Usually so obedient, he ignored them, he had stopped playing, was quietly intent on something. *What's he doing? What's he found?*

I'd better go and see.

She waited, jogging on the spot. After a while he came slowly towards her, holding the dog by its collar. She stared at him, took no more than a skimming glance towards the mere; she didn't want to see.

'Don't come any nearer, love.'

'No, I won't. Is it . . . someone drowned?'

'Yes, I'll wait here. You go and phone the police.'

CHAPTER SIXTEEN

Sergeant Berrow, accompanied by WPC Linda Hart, went to Longley House. It was WPC Hart who had interviewed Margo as the last person to see Violet, and made out the Missing From Home report.

Adelle, too worried about her mother to follow her usual routine, had gone to Longley early; she was the one who had to do the identifying as Margo proclaimed herself too distraught.

'You'd better try and calm her down,' Adelle said brusquely to Ron, who stood about strained and helpless as his wife's histrionics swept around him. 'Don't let's jump to conclusions. There are always accidents happening at the Mere. It could be anyone.'

In the car Sergeant Berrow said, 'I didn't mention it, as your sister was so upset . . .'

Adelle did not look at him, she stared ahead, expressionless. 'Well?'

'We found your mother's handbag up on the Edge, I thought I'd better prepare you.'

'I see.'

At the mortuary Adelle maintained the absolute composure Sergeant Berrow expected of a Saddler. She thanked him minimally when he offered his condolences. There would be a post-mortem, he told her, to establish the cause of death.

'She drowned, didn't she? Or it was the fall,' Adelle said, white-lipped, distant.

'That's what we have to find out, Mrs Kenning, there are procedures—'

'No woman her age could survive that. Procedures. Some common sense answers would be more to the point. If she went missing on Wednesday, do you mean to say her body was in the Mere all yesterday when you were supposed to be *looking* for her?'

'We had no reason to believe she would be in such an unlikely place—'

'And I suppose anyone walking past would think she was a log or something.'

'I doubt anyone walked there yesterday,' Sergeant Berrow said with heavy patience. 'If you recall, it was pouring all day. It would help if you could suggest a reason why your mother should go up there in—'

'There isn't one.' She spoke with such glacial impatience the words *You fool* hung unspoken.

Sergeant Berrow explained courteously that he was extremely busy and WPC Hart would drive her back. He didn't see why he should put up with a woman who insulted him personally and professionally.

People reacted to sudden death with a bewildering diversity of emotion, both Bob Berrow and Linda Hart were experienced enough to make allowances, even so, as he said to her later, 'I wouldn't say she was grieving, angry more like.' Linda agreed that that was her impression—'And when I got back to Longley House, Mrs Duggan was in the porch. Would you believe it, they started yelling at each other before I'd turned the car round. You could still hear them when they went inside.' The Saddlers, Berrow observed sourly, had never been known for pleasantries. His granny told him that it had been well known that if old Joseph couldn't find anyone ready for a row, he'd fall out with the stones in the road.

* * *

Inspector Armstrong scrupulously assembled

and passed on to Hunter everything he could possibly want to know about the incident.

It seemed that on the Wednesday afternoon, Ron Duggan, Margo's husband, drove their two children over to a private hotel called the Gables, on the Clerehaven road, just outside Knutsford. The owners were related to the Saddlers and their daughter was celebrating her eighteenth birthday on the Friday. Several of the youngsters who were the closest relatives had been ferried there the day before in order to lend a hand with the arrangements; although how anyone expected to get anything in the way of help from a bunch of teenagers no one seemed to know.

Later that afternoon Margo had driven her mother into town, dropped her off at the car park behind the Market Square, from where she would make her own way to Ruskin Close to spend the evening with her other daughter, Mrs Adelle Kenning. Thursdays and Saturdays were market days, the town was very busy, it was dusk. Later enquiries had not yet turned up anyone sighting old Mrs Saddler.

Margo went home and busied herself. When her husband returned from the Gables, they took advantage of being free of the family to have a romantic evening together with a candle-lit dinner. They assumed that sometime later Adelle drove her mother home. They slept at the back of the house and wouldn't hear anything. The next morning, Ron went off to work; Mrs Saddler, usually an early bird, was so late coming down to the kitchen for breakfast that Margo went up to her room, found her bed had not been slept in.

She phoned her sister, who was unavailable, left a message, and then contacted everyone she could think of who might know her mother's whereabouts. She became increasingly distressed, eventually went to the police station. She was worried because her mother had lately taken to unaccountable wanderings.

Armstrong himself, accompanied by WPC Hart, interviewed Margo.

When she was asked why her mother should go all the way up to Merlin Edge, she said that she had herself taken her for a drive out there on the Monday, they'd had a flask of tea and biscuits and admired the view. Later, her mother was upset at discovering she had lost her pearls; it could be that she had convinced herself that she had lost them at Merlin Edge and, in a confused way, gone up there to look for them. As it turned out the pearls were not lost; she must have forgotten where she had put them because Margo had since found them in a drawer in her mother's room.

The post-mortem established that Violet had died by drowning, and put her time of death at approximately five p.m., but it yielded nothing conclusive about the manner in which death occurred. Her walking stick was discovered floating in the Mere, her handbag had been found on Merlin Edge, but a thorough search produced nothing significant. She had not been attacked; the area where she could reasonably have been likely to fall down the precipice showed no signs of struggle; the ground was wet and held the impressions of footprints, car and bicycle tyres, but, as it was a well-visited spot, even in autumn, that was to be expected. In the pathologist's opinion there was nothing suspicious about the death but they were awaiting results of toxicology reports, blood samples and analysis of the stomach contents. Unless they revealed something startling, the pathologist thought it unlikely the Coroner would be concerned with what, in his own view, was an accidental death.

Inspector Armstrong, recalling Hunter's previous enquiries, had given thought to the matter, along with Sergeant Berrow's and WPC Hart's observations. 'I could not help wondering, sir, if there's anything at the back of all this.'

Hunter made a sound that could have meant anything; Inspector Armstrong interpreted it as encouragement and went on, 'Well, on the face of it, it's just small time . . . that young woman and her phone calls. I didn't quite see why you . . . well, I wondered—what was there in it to merit your interest?'

Smart arse. But he's right. He's going far,

fast; three or four more years and I'll be calling him 'sir'. Hunter had never been a man to stand in the way of anyone's ambition. He told him, briefly, what he had so far kept to himself—the tenuous connection with Minim's murder.

Armstrong was at once alert. 'This is significant. This isn't some parochial interlude . . . it's a possible link to a major investigation. I'll ask around and see if I can turn anything up.'

Later that day Sergeant Berrow spoke to Inspector Armstrong. He privately regarded him as one of the new breed set to fly high once someone had ignited the rocket in his arse. But that was how things went nowadays. 'Sir, when Mr Hunter first spoke to me about the Saddlers, there was something I didn't think to mention. It didn't occur to me it might be relevant, it might not be, but you said anything that related—'

'I haven't got all day, Bob.'

'No, well it's really just gossip, and I don't—'

'Do gossip. So you frequently tell us. Go on.'

'It was Linda Hart reminded me, you know she handled the misper in the first place and then today—'

'*What*?' Armstrong prompted with savage forbearance.

When Berrow had told him, Armstrong was

silent for a while. 'Right. Give Mr Hunter a ring and tell him.'

'But—I mean—I thought you—'

'No. You. I don't do gossip, Bob.'

No, not from such a humble source, because if anything successful came of it, Armstrong certainly wouldn't want it known his shining career had been helped on its way by a cleaning woman's gossip. It was good enough for Sergeant Berrow, though. And if it turned out to be a waste of time it would all be Berrow's fault.

CHAPTER SEVENTEEN

Annette and Mary Clegg drove to Rush Deeping through a great, high wind that tore through the trees, stripping leaves and sending showers of them down on the road.

'All I can say, for someone who doesn't gossip, Bob Berrow's been digging pretty deep,' Annette observed.

Mary, alert to the point of bursting, said, '*Tell.*'

'We go back a few years. He has a neighbour—'

Mary was ready with her notebook, 'Mrs Betty Rowle, 18 Delamere Road.'

'She worked temporarily as a cleaner at the Saddlers, temporary because her auntie, who usually did the cleaning, had to go into hospital for a hysterectomy. That took quite a while and during that time Betty Rowle, it seems, became embroiled in the domestic life of the Saddlers.'

'How?'

'I'll tell you, but this is just what's been passed on to me through—'

'Mr Hunter.'

'He got it from Bob Berrow. Our priority is to establish a time-scale. If what she has to tell us doesn't tie in with Minim's murder, then it's not worth bothering with, and we drop it. OK?'

* * *

Betty Rowle, plump and neat, welcomed them smilingly. Her house was bright, tidy, her lounge full of cheerful colour and family photos. She expressed a conventional regret of Violet's death that had dignity but, noticeably, little warmth. 'Bob Berrow said I could help you with some information. I must say I can't think how, but I'll do my best. Now, you'd like some coffee.'

'Not just at the moment, thank you,' Annette said politely. 'If you don't mind, if we can just cover the preliminaries, we have another call to make, you see.'

'Yes, you must be very busy,' Betty said seriously, and set about establishing what she called the 'preminaries': why she went to work for the Saddlers, how long, and when. Annette briskly corralled her when her instinct to chat looked like taking over, Mary sat busily quiet with her notebook.

'So. You were there between the middle of Jan to middle of Feb 1986. I understand that during that time you found some bloodstained clothing. Can you remember when that was?'

Betty looked mildly amazed. 'D'you know, I'd forgotten all about that, it was so long ago. I didn't actually *tell* Bob, well, not like reporting it or anything. I'd popped in to see Amy—his wife—and was having a cup of tea and a good moan, and he was there. Fancy him remembering.'

Patiently, Annette pressed her, expecting uncertainty and rambling references, but Betty was at once positive. 'It was after the old man had his stroke. That was on eleventh February.'

Mary said, 'You're very sure, Mrs Rowle.'

'Betty. I'm not likely to forget, it was my Sharon—my daughter's—birthday. She was that proud of being ten—into two figures—and with all that was going on at the Saddlers, I was ever so late back for her party. As it was I had to ring our mam and get her round to start getting things ready—'

'The day Mr Saddler had his stroke was the eleventh?'

'Well, in the night, you know what I mean.

That morning when I turned up, eight o'clock, place was in a turmoil. Ambulance had just been and took him.'

'And this was the day you found the bloodstained clothing?'

'Yes.' Betty frowned, concentrating. 'I'm pretty sure . . . but with everything such a state.'

There was a short silence while Annette considered this and Mary consulted her notebook. The wind battered against the windows of the snug little house; a laburnum in the garden thrashed, bent to breaking point. Annette said, 'I think we've got time for coffee after all, don't you Mary?'

The kitchen opened off the lounge, Betty left the door open, talking. The aroma of freshly baked scones exquisitely accompanied her voice. 'What I can't understand, all this time, how can it interest you?'

Annette went to the open door, said matter-of-factly that it might possibly tie in with an enquiry that had not been cleared up. 'You know we like to tidy up loose ends, even though it's nothing significant.'

'Oh, yes, I know how particlar Bob is. Right stickleton, he is.'

'Exactly,' Annette said, inventing something unalarming. 'Statistics. Accident statistics.'

To her surprise, Betty nodded in prompt agreement. 'Well, yes, I see. Margo did say about the accident, but I have to admit I never did know the ins and outs of it.'

'No,' Annette agreed, with casual interest, turned away to meet Mary's bright gaze. *Yes* . . .

Betty sailed forward, tray bearing.

When they were sitting down, Annette said, 'Let me just get this straight: Wednesday, the eleventh, was a perfectly ordinary day—nothing happened out of the ordinary. Right. So, just for now, Betty, if you'd tell us about the next morning, just how things happened. I'd like to get the details straight.'

'Well, as I said, as I got there, ambulance was just going off with old Mr Saddler, and Mrs Saddler was going to go to the hospital with him. I was a bit surprised to find Margo there—that she'd been there since night before, I mean.'

'Why?' Annette asked.

Betty explained there'd been a big bust up a couple of years before, when Margo and her husband had split up. 'Not that I'd been there then, but I knew about it from Auntie Muriel. Margo'd wanted to come back to Longley then, but her father wouldn't have her. I'm not sure where she'd been living, Chatfield, I think. After a while her mam and dad let her and the children come and visit but they'd never have him—her husband, Ron.'

'So it was unusual for her to stay overnight?'

'Mmm. Unless her kids were with her, but they weren't. They came following week.

Then, just after, Ron moved in. I was a bit surprised, I must say, the old boy had never let him set foot across the doorstep—'

'Right. These scones are absolute heaven. Let's just stick with that morning for now. You stayed at the house to see to your usual work, and Margo was there with you.'

She could not, Betty said tartly, get on with her usual work with the place upside down, Margo almost in hysterics, on the phone every ten minutes to just about everyone. 'Then expecting me to get her some lunch—well, that was never my job, I told her—your mother always sees to that. She tells me she has to have something to eat or she'd collapse from nervous strain . . . I've never seen anyone less like collapsing, I can tell you.'

Eventually Margo went off to the hospital, vociferous on the subject of Adelle, who was nowhere to be found. However, Adelle rang while Betty was alone and Betty had to tell her the news; she accepted it, as she did everything, without fuss and said she would drive straight to the hospital.

Annette mildly queried why Adelle could not be found, wasn't she at work, or at home in Rush Deeping? Betty said no, Adelle had been working and living away somewhere since the previous year, when her marriage had broken up. She'd decided to return to Rush Deeping and buy a house and had been in and out of Longley on several occasions during the negotiations, most of the time she came up she stayed with a friend in Chatfield.

'Margo told me not to leave the house till someone came back from the hospital, but it was getting that late, seemed so cold-hearted just to go. First sight of them I was off, last minute for my little girl's party, but there you are, I made it.'

'But it was that day you found the bloodstained clothes?' Annette said.

'Yes, yes.'

'What happened?'

'Margo was hard at something when I got there; I must say I was surprised to see her shift herself. Usually just sits about wanting to be waited on. But there she was, busy going in and out of the back with buckets and cloths. I came on this pile of clothes in the back utility room, next to the laundry basket. I went to pick them up to put in washer and I'd only just noticed all these stains, bloodstains.'

Mary asked, 'You were sure they were bloodstains?'

Betty said wryly, 'I've brought up four lads, I know bloodstains when I see them. And any road, some came off on me hands, when I unfolded them, like. Then Margo comes in, and like a whirlwind, snatches them off of me, shouting what was I doing with them.'

From that point there were high words and confusion. Margo said there had been an accident that had occurred the night her father had had his stroke. 'She said I hadn't to say nothing about the clothes to Mr and Mrs Saddler—not that he'd understand anything—but she didn't want her mother upset any more than she was. Then she goes off, all dramatical and it struck me—she must have been cleaning their car. I didn't ask, she wasn't going to have me cleaning cars on top of everything else.'

'Cleaning her parents' car?'

'Well . . . maybe there was a mess, if it had been in an accident—' Betty paused, sighed. 'I never had the rights of that. To be honest, I thought the old boy had had a drop too much and shouldn't have been driving. Mind you—that's just what I thought, I'm not saying it was so. And now he's gone, and old Mrs Saddler. None of it made much sense to me, they were never ones for going out at night, Mr Saddler couldn't see all that well and Mrs Saddler couldn't drive—'

'How do you know it was night?'

'Well, Margo said something about the weather all to do with the accident. It'd been a terrible night that Wednesday, black as pitch and pouring rain, flooding all round about. She'd meant to get to Rush Deeping early but she was held up because of being diverted, and they'd only just got back . . .'

'She didn't go into details about the accident?'

'None as I could follow,' Betty said dryly. 'And no one else saw fit to mention it, not far as I know. Tell the truth, I give up the job not long after. I didn't want to let me auntie down, but she was really poorly after her operation, and decided to give up herself. Madame Margo and Ron and their kids moved in, so Mrs Saddler had plenty of support. Dot Beddoes went to work for them. She's as bad tempered as they are, suit each other.'

Mary reached for another scone. 'Fall out a lot, did they?'

'You've never come across such a family. Old feller, before he had his stroke, always shouting and bullying. Mrs Violet—she was just, well, a quiet, ordinary lady. Always had that edge, mind—that she was so much better than anyone. But in her own way she gave him as good as she got. The girls went at each other hammer and tongs, but when she said "jump" they didn't half jump.'

Annette asked casually, 'Did you ever come across their son—Ian, I think he was called.'

'Oh, yes, he'd come and visit,' Betty said matter-of-fact. That's what families were about, in her experience: keeping in touch, visiting, being concerned with each other's doings. 'But why he bothered, I don't know, it was like a red rag to a bull. Couldn't be half an hour with his father before the old man got into such a rage it's a wonder he didn't have poplexity.'

'What was he like?' Annette asked. 'Ian?'

'Like?'

'Yes,' Annette said encouragingly, 'How would you describe him?'

Betty struggled with the simple human failing of being unable to describe anyone and eventually settled for: just ordinary, just an ordinary youngster.

Mary tried. 'Would you say he was a typical Saddler?'

'Oh, no. Bit sort of shy. But polite, had a smile and something cheerful to say. To me, at any rate. Different matter among themselves, not that anyone could get much of a word in when the old feller started.'

'What exactly did he have against Ian?' Annette asked.

'Blowed if I know. Shouted at him stuff about artists, and being deng—gent—indent.' Betty gave up.

'Ungentlemanly?' Annette ventured; in view of Betty's creative way with words, it could have been anything.

'Don't think so. I've seen the poor lad go away in tears. You wouldn't do it to your own, would you? No matter what.'

'How did the rest of the family treat him?' Mary asked.

'Well, Adelle isn't one for showing her feelings much, but she did chat away to him quietly sometimes. Margo just turned her back on him, as if he wasn't there. Mrs Saddler—nothing put her out, never raised her voice, or took anyone's side as I could tell. She'd come in the passage and tell me to move that great chest and vac behind it, as if nothing was happening—and all the while the old man was yelling at Ian in the lounge. You'd think a mother . . . Oh, well, we're not all made the same, are we?'

'Just as well,' Annette murmured. 'Can you remember the last time you saw Ian?'

'Yes, it was the Monday. There was a hell of a row, it got so I couldn't stand it, went and shut myself in the pantry. Then he went off and two nights later—well that was when his father had the stroke.'

And the *accident*, Annette added silently. 'Did he come and visit his father while he was ill?'

'If he did, it wasn't as I know, but then, I said, I didn't stay more than a month. He might have, and I never saw him—well, it was a time for family to rally round, in spite of their differences, so he could have done.'

A silent consensus: rallying round was just about the last thing that family would do.

Mary asked, 'Have you ever seen him since then?'

'No. I know he never turned up for the old feller's funeral because there was talk about that. People notice. Can't say I was all that surprised, though.'

Annette did an interior checklist, took a chance. 'He seems to have disappeared, doesn't he?'

'Well, I wouldn't know. Only ever came across him all that time ago. And it's not as if we were congenial, you know.'

'I know,' Annette said, deciding not to bother with that one.

'And only thing I've ever heard since was some while back—but I put it down to just kids' talk—about him making monymous phone calls.'

'Yes, we know about those,' Annette said, very carefully.

'Do you?' Betty looked mildly surprised.

'How did you hear about them?'

'Well, that's it—kids. I thought it was just one of those zaggerating things they get up to. My Sharon's at school with Charmian—that's Margo's daughter, and she had some tale about these phone calls and her mam said it'd be her uncle Ian because he wasn't right in the head. But he never struck *me* as being ninepence to the shilling, and I told my Sharon, "Don't you go talking around like that, it's not nice, and it's labelling people." And that Charmian's a right—' Betty halted, suddenly aghast, 'You don't think it was me? That's not why you're here—what you're checking up on—'

Mary said, 'Betty, if you had something to say you'd come straight out with it, wouldn't you? You're not capable of doing anything anonymous.' Betty's hand was somewhere in the region of her heart. She said breathlessly,

‘No, honestly, I wouldn’t—and my Sharon wouldn’t, she’s good as gold when I impressure on her. She hasn’t been saying things . . .’

Between them, Annette and Mary reassured her, wound her down gradually, tied up some loose ends, and left.

On the drive back they were silent for some time, then Mary said, ‘She’s got the date bang on by fixing it with her daughter’s birthday, the night of Joseph Saddler’s stroke . . .’

‘The night of Minim’s murder,’ Annette finished for her.

‘She can’t stand the Saddlers, all right, but she wouldn’t make things up, would she? I don’t read her as that type, and I don’t think she’s capable of it, do you?’

‘No.’

After another silence Mary said, a question in her voice, ‘Those bloodstained clothes. That was the day after.’

‘Yes . . . But the house was in a turmoil, people overlook things—we should know that. It’s still all a puzzle, though.’

‘Mr Hunter’ll sort it out,’ Mary said confidently.

CHAPTER EIGHTEEN

Hunter and Annette drove to Rush Deeping the following morning. It was as if the winds had exhausted the day and left it settled into a melancholy stillness, a thick, grey lack of light.

They turned off High Martinsgate and followed the drive past Sandy's bungalow, through the rigid avenue of evergreens, round to the stone steps and dark tiles of the side entrance. It was here, in earlier years, carriages would stop to deposit their passengers before driving on to the out-of-sight stables. If there had once been raked gravel and tended garden, now this nether region of the house had a hopeless look, lank shrubs and a concreted area let on to a yard containing a battered red Metro, a slick-looking Audi Quattro. They parked, took a slow look round. 'Seen better days,' Annette murmured.

'Aren't they supposed to have money?'

'They don't believe in spending it. According to Betty the old man was dead against anything new-fangled, and Mrs Saddler didn't believe in show.'

Ron, sharply well-dressed, opened the door to them. When they introduced themselves the smile on his narrow face slowly re-formed into a more suitable gravity. Nervously shrugging, he led them into a dim, narrow hallway that disappeared into a distance of more narrow hallway and showed them into the lounge. Before a gas fire, a colourful figure in the half light, in bulgingly tight red jersey and green plaid trousers, Margo's voluptuous bulk posed on a rather battered looking sofa; the air was saturated with her cloggingly sweet scent. To Annette's amusement she was wearing dark glasses, which must have made it difficult to see in the gloom.

She responded to Hunter's formal expression of condolence with an air of dramatic distraction, said things about being under great stress but she would do her best to help, although she had no idea what more she could do.

'Please, sit down.' Indicating a hefty armchair beside the settee. She glanced once at Annette and then ignored her. Annette sat in an armchair too massive to be moved closer. Ron hovered.

With repetitive variations that she would do *everything in her power* to assist him, Margo's manner became less restrained, hinting at an intimacy so inappropriate it made Annette blink. She flapped a hand in her husband's direction. 'Ron, go and make those phone calls.' He hesitated; she turned to look at him, dark glasses eclipsing any expression on her face. 'And turn the light on on your way.' He shuffled, shrugged, went away, switching on the light by the door.

Curiously, it was an overhead fluorescent strip. The room sprang under its glare—shabby and ponderous, booby-trapped by silver trophies and rosettes, endless dog photographs; a cavernous fireplace of black marble where the old style gas fire hissed.

Margo inclined towards Hunter, 'He's so protective—but I have to show him I'm strong. And I know you'll understand. It might be better if we spoke privately.'

Hunter gave Annette a companionable glance, said with a heartiness only she knew had *danger* written all round it, 'In professional partnerships like ours, we do our job all the better in pairs, Mrs Duggan.'

'Well, yes, in the ordinary run of things, but when discretion is important,' she inclined further, her voice low, 'rapport can be so . . . rewarding.'

'Can it?' Hunter said conversationally.

Her full red lips curved. 'Oh, yes, a—personal—approach; the murmur accompanied by a slight, dismissive movement of her head in Annette's direction.

Annette's inner being quivered with hysterical disbelief. *You're wasting your time with him, you old raunch bag. And do you really think you can get rid of me the way you got rid of your husband?*

Hunter, who had been giving the 'personal approach' some thought, said, 'Has its risks.'

'What's life without risks?'

'Depends what they are. For instance, it obviously doesn't apply in the present circumstances, but when a policeman interviews an attractive lady,' he paused. She leaned closer. Annette wondered if the sofa was stable enough not to capsize.

'—if he isn't accompanied by a colleague, well, there's always the danger someone might get the impression he's trying to take advantage. It has been known, I don't deny it. It would be all too easy, he's in a position of trust, she's vulnerable, and of course, if she's good-looking . . . But, as I said, that doesn't apply here. But on the other hand—he continued, with all the deliberation of a wart-hog wading very slowly through mud, 'it can happen, *has* happened—circumstances might lead to the impression the officer *might* be trying to take advantage—or even be under the mistaken impression that he's been *offered* an advantage, you know, some kind of trading for favours.' He shook his head slowly, making tutting noises. 'No, as I said, none of that applies in this situation . . . But, hasn't that so often been the case DC Jones?'

'Yes, sir,' Annette said, inflexibly on parade.

Margo said, 'Er . . .'

'You are *quite right*. My colleague and I do agree that the best recourse now is to proceed along accepted . . .' He continued, ploddingly playing the crude cop she had taken him for, turning her tactic back on her. Her totally baffled air indicated it would be some time before she worked it out.

'Now, if you'd like to tell me the circumstances when you last saw your mother.'

As if she could not quite believe such a detached response, Margo, at last retrieving her ego, said coaxingly, 'Oh, I've been through all that, time and again—'

'Yes. And if you'll just tell me, my colleague will take notes.'

Margo spared Annette a glare. 'What in God's name for? And I might remind you, *I'm* the one who reported my mother missing—'

Annette said, 'We frequently find that people overlook details without realising their relevance. Just going over what happened, sometimes an everyday association sparks off a recollection . . .' She could talk platitudes for a long time, long enough for Margo to lose patience.

'Oh, *all right* . . .'

It was a histrionic account, concluding on a truculent note. 'Now, look here, as a family we should be left to mourn in decent privacy—*and* I've got the funeral to arrange, it's no good asking my sister, she's always much too busy with her own concerns. As far as your lot are concerned I've done *nothing* but answer questions and what I *deserve* is to be told exactly what's happening.'

So Hunter told her, in grinding detail, the

procedures that were necessary in a case of accidental death, the steps that were being taken, by whom, when. Long before he had finished, her attention wandered. She took off her dark glasses and wafted them at him. Her darting eyes, heavily made up, showed no sign of weeping.

'That's all very well. What I can't understand is why someone didn't see her going up to the Edge. That's what you should be trying to find out, ask people. I could make an appeal on television—'

'It's all right, Mrs Duggan, we've got that in hand with the local press and radio.'

'I could tell everyone how vulnerable she'd become, wandering off. I've a cousin who has a bookshop in town, it's not long since she got in touch with me because Mother had wandered in there in a confused state.'

Hunter said, 'I understand you have a brother, Mrs Duggan.'

She stared at him. 'Ian? What? Yes. What's he got to do with this?'

'Have you seen him recently.'

'*Ian*. Not for years.' It was difficult to tell if she was being grudging or guarded.

Annette said helpfully, 'Ah, years, they pass so quickly, don't they? How long, would you say?'

'*I* don't know, what does it matter? Five years. You should be finding out about what happened to a helpless old lady—'

‘Oh, so he doesn’t live in Rush Deeping.’

‘No. And before you ask, I’ve no idea where he lives. If you must know, he was never one of the family, although what our private affairs are to do with you, I don’t know. When he was a kid he went away to live with an aunt in Chatfield, because Mother was ill and couldn’t cope with him, and he just never wanted to come back home.’

‘So you lost touch. What about your sister?’

‘What about her?’ Margo said, blankly.

‘Did your brother keep in touch with her?’

‘How should *I* know. I’ve no idea what she gets up to.’

‘I understand,’ Annette said mildly, ‘that a short time ago you were troubled by anonymous phone calls.’

‘*What?*’ She glared, gave a sudden shake of her head, swept her arm out. ‘That was something Mother dreamed up, she’d begun to imagine all kinds of things lately. Losing her pearls, for instance . . .’ She told them, with many repetitions and occasional barks of derisive laughter, about the ‘missing’ pearls being in her mother’s dressing table drawer all the time. ‘Look, that radio appeal—why don’t I do it—’

‘It’s kind of you to offer, but it’s all under way, I wouldn’t want to put you to any trouble at a time like this. Thank you for your help. Good day.’ Hunter was up and leaving in long, rapid strides, Annette immediately following.

Behind them, Margo had the curiously deflated look of a balloon from which the air was slowly leaking.

Ron loitered along the narrow hall. He had all the blatant honesty of someone who had been listening at the door. 'She's very upset, has mood swings, it's understandable. She's extremely sensitive . . . well, you'll have realised that. You mustn't take too much notice of what she says . . .'

It wasn't until they were in the car and halfway down the drive Annette said, 'Whew.'

'Right on . . .' He drove in silence, eventually pulled up in an elegant oval of truly splendid houses, threaded by spaces of massive shrubs and old trees, the grisaille light haunted by nannies and privileged tots, women elegantly strolling, the clop of horses' hooves . . .

They had to shake themselves, unravel the time warp.

Annette didn't need to say it: *that godawful woman was coming on to you.* Since she had worked with him, Annette had known Hunter fall in love twice, once with a woman much younger than himself, one older: clever, sparkling, warm women, who had nothing in common with Margo's slovenly sexuality. The point was—did Margo habitually proffer herself to anyone she fancied? Or did she have an ulterior motive . . . getting him on her side? In that case, she was making a grievous mistake.

Annette said, 'Ron doesn't like the law.'

'Ron the Con, I believe he's known as. Not that we've had him for anything . . . yet. Did you notice, there was one photograph of the older Saddlers' wedding—everything else was bloody dogs. Something tells me they weren't sentimentally attached to family snaps.'

'No, well, why have photos of people you dislike. She was very keen to do a Zsa Zsa Gabor act, wasn't she? Dark glasses, publicity.'

Hunter murmured agreement, their shared thought: if this woman is so intent on engineering a drama, what else has she engineered?

Annette said, 'And what's the truth about Ian? According to her he never wanted to come home. According to Sandy's mother—and Betty—he kept trying to re-establish a relationship.'

'Yes. And trying to pass the anonymous phone calls off as her mother's delusion. I don't believe a word she said. Either she's got something to hide, or she's a fantasist, and they always believe their own lies.'

They had earlier agreed he would use his judgement about the accident and the bloodstained clothes. His instinct and his training was to keep it to himself, in accordance with the accepted wisdom: when in doubt, keep your trap shut and listen. Information is power. And until he had pursued other avenues, built up a clearer picture—the wrong move and everything could go pear-shaped.

He looked at his watch, started the car. 'I want something in the way of corroboration. There's only one person who's part of the family and sounds like a reasonable human being.'

CHAPTER NINETEEN

It took subtlety to call a bookshop Rush, when in its soft enfolding calm nothing more urgent occurred than low-voiced conversation, silent communion with loved authors, mute mental wrestling with difficult subjects, negotiations of diffidence and quiet good nature.

Hunter had last seen Dorcas Grey in her Chatfield shop almost two years before; he remembered a small, finely made woman with an elfin face, friendly smile, warm brown eyes. She was just the same, in jeans and oversize jersey, on top of a ladder, stowing books on a high shelf. She smiled happily at Annette, disposed of the last volume, shinned down the ladder, landing with a little jump. 'Hallo, nice to see you.'

'Hallo, Dorcas. This is my boss, Detective Chief Inspector Hunter.'

Dorcas studied their warrant cards for a long moment before saying, 'OK. You got me bang to rights. I done the blag.'

Annette smothered a laugh, Hunter said kindly, 'I think you've been watching too much television. We just have a few questions—'

Her small hand flew to her mouth. 'Oh, it's about Mrs Saddler, isn't it? I'm so sorry, that was crass. I don't mean to sound—' She stopped, confused, looked around the shop. 'I haven't been here long, there's so much to do, and I've got a new house, and that's . . . what I mean is, I'm so taken up with myself, I forget there's a world outside. And this awful thing's happened in it . . .' She gathered her apology together, polite, restrained—after all, they had been related—then herded them towards her office, signalled to her assistant in the back reaches. He appeared, a big, grey-haired, smiling man. 'Vic, be a dear and mind the store while I talk to the fuzz.'

Without a word from him, she added, 'Coffee, yes, ta.' Leaving Hunter and Annette with the shared impression of a semaphore system perfected over time to keep noise down and counteract distance, bookstands and odd corners.

In the office, they cleared themselves spaces to sit from teetering piles of books, Annette admired a stack of antique framed Cheshire maps while Hunter studied all the papers he could see on Dorcas's desk with the innocent observation, 'How do you keep it so tidy? I've never managed to clear the wreckage off mine.

Your assistant. Your husband?'

'No. Old chum. Took early retirement from teaching. *Mad* about books, helps out part time.'

'You don't mind if Annette takes notes.'

'Gosh, this is official,' Dorcas breathed. A pause in the casual everyday, a rethinking of positions. 'I just don't know what I can tell you.'

'Well, let's start with your concern about Mrs Saddler wandering in here in a confused condition. I understand you had to phone the family to have her collected from—'

'Hang on, hang on,' Dorcas, perplexed, interrupted. 'She never set foot in here as far as I know. Margo was in here, about three weeks ago. She said if Violet turned up, would I . . . Don't say it was Margo who told you . . .' She stopped, exasperated. After thought she said consideringly, almost distantly, 'She's such a bloody liar. I suppose I shouldn't say that.'

'We had worked it out for ourselves,' Annette said. 'But why should she say that if it wasn't true?'

'Margo doesn't have to have a reason for saying anything. Whatever comes into her head.'

They asked if she had any idea why Mrs Saddler would go up to the Edge alone but she was as baffled as everyone else; she had had no contact with her for several weeks.

Vic edged his way into the small, crowded

space, carrying a tray around which a delicious aroma floated.

Dorcas arranged mugs, milk, sugar. 'Vic, did Mrs Saddler ever come in while I was out?'

'Not that I saw.'

'You knew her?' Hunter asked.

'By sight. No one Rush born and bred could overlook the Saddlers.' The shop bell jangled, he said, 'Must watch the stock,' and went out.

Annette said, 'D'you remember, when I first came to see you here, you told me something about the Saddlers receiving anonymous phone calls.'

Dorcas thought for a moment, nodded. 'Oh, yes, that was the kids, wasn't it?' She halted—the delayed realisation of the innately trusting. 'Hey . . . did you . . . ? Was that why you were asking about . . . ? Were you here officially, *then*?'

Annette hunched up, whispered, '*Mea culpa*.'

'Not only that, she's guilty,' Hunter said.

'Do you mean there really *was* something in that business of anonymous . . . *Good God*, you don't think it was me.'

Annette tried not to smile. The second thoroughly decent person with an appalled reaction. How many more? Only Margo had dismissed the matter as insignificant.

'No,' Hunter said carefully. 'But, there seemed to be some suspicion it was Ian.'

Dorcas blinked. 'Ian? Has he turned up?'

'Is there any reason why he shouldn't?' Hunter asked.

'Well, I suppose . . .' An embarrassed pause. 'As his mother's died it would be . . . well, quite the normal sort of thing . . .'

'But?'

'Honestly, I don't know.' She drank her coffee.

After a silence, Hunter said, 'He never came to his father's funeral, did he? He doesn't get on with the family.'

'You could put it like that.'

'When did you last see him?'

'Not for years . . .' She did some inward calculations. 'It was when I still had the shop in Manchester . . . I sold that in the spring of eighty-eight. But he hadn't been around for . . . oh, a couple of years before that.'

'So you last saw him in nineteen eighty-six, would you say?'

'Mmm . . . Probably. Is it important?' She had come to a halt, polite, wary.

'It might be,' Annette said. 'There's some information we need and we could possibly get it, indirectly, this way.'

Dorcas regarded her sceptically. 'All right, if you say so.'

Hunter drew back imperceptibly. There were ways women could speak to each other—nuanced, sympathetic; times when their communication was so instinctive his male presence was crashing. He made himself still, drank his excellent coffee, listened.

Annette said, 'Ian's family don't appear to know or care where he is or what he's doing.'

'They never have, it's no secret. Unpleasant, but true.'

'But he kept in touch with you?'

'On and off. He lived in Chatfield, I had a shop in Chatfield, I was rather a sitting duck.'

Annette asked, 'Did he often come into your shop?'

Dorcas said rather wryly that he did when it suited his purpose and for a while there were two. 'One was to get away from a girl—so he said.'

'Did he tell you her name?' Annette asked.

'Yes.' Dorcas looked at them in turn. 'Why do I know you already know it? Oh, well. Sandy. You're not looking for her as well, are you?'

'No, we know where she is. She hasn't seen Ian for a long while, she seems to think there's something odd about his disappearance.'

'Well, she would, wouldn't she? He had every intention of dropping her, the only way he could do it was to make himself scarce.'

'You think that's why he just—disappeared?'

'Oh, he was always wandering off after some new craze, then giving up, wandering back. His father forced him to go into computers as a career and it infuriated him when Ian chucked it all.'

'Everyone's going into computers now.

Total nerds,' Annette said philosophically.

'That's true. Technology was the last thing Ian could cope with, with his artistic temperament.'

An imperceptible pause before Hunter asked, with feline delicacy, 'He paints?'

'He did when I last saw him, it's probably something else now. Although, I don't know, it did seem to mean so much to him . . .' She stopped, following a private thought.

Since Hunter said nothing, Annette prompted. 'Did he talk to you about it?'

'Never stopped. That's the other reason he came in my shop. I've always had a pretty good art section, he haunted it for what? two or three years. And then, suddenly . . . Oh, I suppose it was bound to turn to manure. Everything else did.'

Hunter, 'Everything?'

'Yes,' Dorcas said, and explained. Poetry, fashion design, acting, sculpture—flamboyant enthusiasms into which Ian threw himself with the fervour of the self-deceived. This was the *only* course his life could take, this was his destiny . . .

But he came from a family whose collective mind was strait-jacketed, to them such wild terrain signalled the socially dubious—if not downright insane. But he—wilfully or unconsciously—could never accept they had no common ground. In all his efforts to prove himself he compensated for their rejection by throwing down a challenge: *I can make it in spite of you.* But he never did, he gave up, lost interest, set off in another direction. Painting was, as far as Dorcas knew, the last direction.

And the irony was, he was getting somewhere with it—so he claimed. He always anticipated his triumphs—and had very good excuses when they didn't materialise. But she had believed this time was different, his artistic talent was so focused upon on his need to be valued by his family it could all have been true—a dealer selling his paintings, the exhibition—or was it private view?

'Private view? When?' Hunter asked.

'Sorry, I don't know. It was about the time I lost touch with him. I don't know if it ever happened.'

'Did he say where it was? Can you remember anything he told you about it?' Annette asked.

They waited in encouraging silence while she searched her memory.

'A gallery somewhere in Chatfield. There are millions. It would have been sometime early spring. He was so wired up about it—he got that way about all his crazes, and honestly, this one was mega boring—'

For Hunter an echo from the long unsolved investigation, Jocelyn Prendergast's voice, *It's enormously important for an artist to get his work exhibited—*

'—he said at the right time everyone would

know about it, so I thought "OK. I'll wait," and just didn't take any more notice. He'd sworn me to secrecy, apparently secrecy was somehow vital—I never worked out why. What was sad, he'd convinced himself his parents would be pleased with his success. This was to be his crowning moment—he was going to invite them to come along and share it.'

Annette said hesitantly, 'But was that the sort of thing they . . . I mean . . .'

'Of course it wasn't, but he wouldn't listen, and I didn't want to be a complete wet blanket. So I just left him to get on with it.'

Vic put his head round the door, 'Dorcas, could you spare a minute?'

She went out to the shop. Hunter and Annette talked quietly for a while: *Minim's murder was all over Chatfield—she had her business there. Wouldn't she put two and two together?—Not necessarily. As she said, there are millions of galleries.—And Ian was such a no-hoper there need have been no truth in anything he told her . . .*

They left, asking her to get in touch if she thought of anything. She regarded them carefully. 'I can't make anything of this. No point in asking, I suppose. No, thought not.' And as they went out of the door she murmured in total bewilderment, 'Why in God's name would Ian want to make anonymous calls. What *for*?'

CHAPTER TWENTY

Outside, Hunter handed Annette the car keys; if he wanted her to drive it meant he needed to immerse himself in his thoughts.

They arrived back in Chatfield without a word, then Hunter said, 'We need to pinpoint the last positive sighting of Ian. And the nearest we've come to that is the address Sandy gave us.'

At Sandy's name Annette groaned softly.

'Yes, for what it's worth. Mary can ask her the date, she's the only one who can get anything approaching coherence out of her. Then, your job, get on to Brighton, see what they can find out for us.' He went away saying darkly, 'What's the betting it's going to be Menlove Gardens all over again.'

Later, in the canteen, Annette was giving her dinner hearty attention when an amiable voice said, 'That's right, bonny lass like you needs to keep up your strength.'

It was community policeman George Withers.

'George, sit down—' He settled his mug of tea and comforting teddy bear presence opposite her. 'Has Mr Hunter talked to you about this Saddler business?' She was sure he had, George was Hunter's oldest friend.

'We've chewed it over a bit. How's it going?'

She told him about the bloodstained clothing and the date coinciding with Minim's murder, then about her Brighton query. 'What does Menlove Gardens mean?'

'East.'

'George, you start this bloody gnomic uttering and I'll throw stones at you. It's bad enough trying to work out—'

'The Julia Wallace murder.'

'What?'

'Nineteen thirties. Liverpool. She was at home alone, found beaten to death. Or was she stabbed? I forget. Anyway, husband established his alibi by claiming he had a telephone message from a man who wanted to see him about some insurance. The address the man gave—according to husband—was Menlove Gardens East. Husband conspicuously asking the way, getting on and off trams—people went about in them then—during the time his wife was getting done in. He never found Menlove Gardens East because there was no such place. He went to trial, but got off. That's about it, I think.'

'Thanks.' Annette was silent for a while. 'It doesn't *help*, does it?'

'No,' George agreed placidly.

* * *

Hunter, Collier and Annette were in one of the Frog and Nightgowns, an unassuming building in a side-street, bypassed by the heedless. The loud and the brash and the modern slipped away as regulars drank companionably in the lingering margin of its Victorian era: mahogany and brass, moulded plaster and decorated glass.

It was Annette who asked. Hunter had no doubt they had conferred, speculated, drawn a deep breath—'Guv, do you think Ian painted Casements? Do you think he murdered Minim?'

He could scarcely claim his thoughts were in order; there had been, for some time, an inchoate process, during which he had been cautious about putting anything into words, even inside his head. But now was as good a time as any.

'Did Ian paint Casements? I have no idea. We have second-hand knowledge—Dorcas—that he was to have what she understood to be an exhibition. We have no idea if this happened, when it happened, or where—except it was most probably in Chatfield. There is a tenuous, so far unverifiable, link with the private view when Minim was murdered. Ian had visited the Gallery with Archie Barnes and therefore must have known Minim. What else?'

They sat thoughtfully. Collier said, 'Sandy's evidence.'

Hunter said, 'I've had more meaningful conversations with pot plants. Sandy grew up with Ian and interpreted their relationship on her own, entirely daft, terms. What evidence?'

Collier hesitated. '*The Man in the Fog*.'

Hunter sighed.

Annette said, 'Come on, guy, she just isn't the type to know—much less conjure up—an extract from an obscure poet.'

Collier said, 'I doubt she knows *any* poetry. You said her stepfather told her the verse was stuck on the back of the painting. That wouldn't normally mean a thing to her. She can quote it because it was one of Ian's favourites.'

'Sandy didn't know that Ian painted, did she?' Annette asked.

'Sandy only knows what's going on inside her head. There doesn't have to be a connection with reality,' Hunter said.

The bulk of George Withers loomed, not only smart in his civvies but impressively masculine. Annette regarded him appreciatively. James said, 'You don't half look sartorial, George. Something special on?'

George said, 'I'm hoping for a night of forbidden passion.'

Annette said, 'Don't wind him up. You know he's susceptible to older men.'

George smiled largely behind his pint. 'Where are we up to?'

'Coincidence,' James volunteered. 'The night Minim is murdered, Ian disappears, so does the painting *The Man in the Fog*, Fayne has never surfaced again. That same night, over at Rush Deeping, after an unexplained "accident", Joseph Saddler suffers a stroke. Daily woman claims that next day his daughter Margo is busy swabbing out a car—cars? And there's a pile of bloodstained clothing in the house.'

'Yes, Annette told me. And, to date, you haven't asked the daughter—Margo—to explain.'

Hunter said nothing, looked inscrutable. Annette said, 'He does that.'

'Has to keep you on your toes. And you know well enough you need room to manoeuvre. She sounds pretty unreliable, put her on guard and you don't know which way she'll jump. What about the daily woman, will she keep things to herself?'

'Sure to. She had too much of a fright about the possibility of libel, and I told her if she wanted to talk, to talk to Bob Berrow.'

'George, you were first on the scene on the night of the murder, weren't you?' James said.

'Yes.' He talked about it, recollections, impressions. Annette and James listened, vicariously present at an unknown incident.

Annette said, 'Terry Bale was there. He said he thought he'd heard talk that Fayne had turned up after all. But there's nothing in the file, no one made a statement to that effect.'

George said, 'No, I know. I remember that rumour at the time. Someone is supposed to have said it was Minim himself who claimed Fayne had been there after all. But who said it?' he shrugged. 'Then again, Minim was known for being a tease.'

'But as it was a rumour, and can't be attributed to anyone it isn't evidence, is it?'

'Hearsay evidence, and where can we get with that?'

Annette said, 'Let's just assume that he did turn up, and that Fayne and Ian were the same person. Then the only possible explanation is that Archie left before he arrived—or vice versa.'

'Yes,' James said. 'For heaven's sake, Ian had been in and out of Archie's house for years, he was his stepdaughter's close friend. I mean, how could he not recognise him—short of Ian turning up at the private view in Groucho Marx spectacles and moustache, or a gorilla suit . . .'

George shook his head. 'No, with that mad crowd no one would have taken the slightest notice.'

'Ergo—Ian wasn't there.'

The silence was short and glum. George said, 'By the way, Annette, your Brighton query. The local lads tracked it down, they left a message for you.'

Some gentle seismic movement in him made her narrow her gaze. 'Well?'

'A ground floor flat in Sebastion Mansions was let to a Mrs Adelle Kenning for a year,

March nineteen eighty-five to March nineteen eighty-six.'

'Stap me vitals,' Annette said.

'Ah,' Hunter said. 'The high-handed bitch, I think was your description.'

'Yes.' She seized a small victory. 'So it wasn't Menlove Gardens. East. After all, Sebastion Mansions exists.'

Collier said impatiently, 'But—nineteen eighty-five to six—that was when *Ian* was supposed to be there—according to Sandy.'

Hunter murmured, '*And the crooked shall be made straight and the rough edges plain.*'

George Withers took this in his confident, everyday stride; 'Isaiah. *That which is crooked cannot be made straight and that which is wanting cannot be numbered.*'

'Ecclesiastes,' Hunter said.

George lifted his pint, said apologetically, 'We had God-fearing mothers.'

* * *

The bell rang. Adelle opened the door to the quiet of Ruskin Close.

There, beyond the figure in the porch, her beloved Rush Deeping unfolded. Everything it meant to her: her esteem, her reputation, her social status, everything she had won as a despised daughter, a striving, clever woman. Everything threatened by the hesitant voice, 'Adelle . . .'

Her face expressionless, she made a small sound, looked quickly outwards—left, right. Said, resigned, 'Oh, come in, for God's sake.'

CHAPTER TWENTY-ONE

Hunter, with Annette, paid a second call to Longley House. It was the first frost of winter; with the sudden drop in temperature the trees had shed their leaves in great drifts and litters. In the gardens the crust of hoar covered lawns and fences and garage roofs.

This time, rather than risk being seen by a wildly overreacting Sandy, (he had no idea if every day was taken up at St. Hilda's) he parked at the front gate. They walked up the path between the snatching, overgrown shrubs to the dark porch; a sideways view of the large lounge window, uncurtained, gave glimpses of ladders, dust sheets.

Mrs Beddoe opened the door. In answer to Annette's query if Mrs Duggan was in she said accusingly, 'There's decorators everywhere,' then went stamping off, leaving them to shut the door and follow.

She disappeared alarmingly round corners; they sprinted in pursuit, Annette muttering, 'This is like Alice after the White Rabbit.' She was right—with the narrow, windowless passages, closed doors, colourless décor—they might just as well have been underground. The central heating had not been turned on, the brisk sparkle of the day seeped through as a clammy chill.

Mrs Beddoe jerked her head, said, 'In there,' and tramped on.

The door opened before they could knock. Margo said, 'What the hell are you doing here?'

'Your daily woman—' Hunter began.

'Oh, her.' Margo peered down the deserted passage.

'You can't get decent staff these days. I suppose you'd better come in.'

They followed the dense block of her perfume into a large, cluttered room, with a depressing view of asbestos garages and half demolished stable, the air was stale and thick, obviously all the heating had been concentrated here. Margo's manner was inappropriately grand. She sat in a heavy, carved chair, facing the unlit, ash-choked fireplace, patted the arms of the chair and explained, 'I've rescued this from the dining room, it was Mother's favourite. We're having both the reception rooms redecorated.'

They found seats for themselves. Hunter's eye was caught by a doll's house, a perfect Queen Anne in miniature, shoved disregarded with an assortment of objects in a corner. When her voice ran down, and she sighed gustily, heavy with meaning, he said, 'Mrs

Duggan, you told us that your cousin rang you from her shop because your mother had gone there without any reason.'

'Cousin? Shop? I did?'

'It wasn't correct, was it? *You* went in there to—'

'Strictly speaking, she's not really a cousin—'

'It was you who went in there to tell her you were concerned about—'

'She probably got it wrong. How can you expect me to remember anything when I'm under all this stress. Anyway, what does it matter?'

'Perhaps it doesn't. What I would like you to explain is the accident your parents had on the night of February the twelfth 1986.'

Rattle her cage, see which way she jumps, Annette thought. The face remained expressionless but the small eyes darted, the fleshy body took on an abrupt tension.

A ringing laugh, 'Accident?' When Hunter didn't reply, she laughed again, 'Where did you hear that?'

'What sort of an accident was it?'

'I don't know. Who's been talking to you?'

Annette repeated the date, adding quietly, 'It was the night your father had a stroke.'

Margo glared at her, after a silence put her hand to her forehead. 'Oh, that . . .' and with some drama began a lengthy, muddled account about her father being ill all day, her mother phoning to ask her to come over, the terrible stormy drive there, the ambulance, eventually, looking sharply at Hunter, 'I suppose it was Adelle told you. Though why she should, I can't—'

'I've not spoken to your sister,' Hunter said. 'Are you saying your father was taken ill during the day?'

'What's it to you? Fat lot of good trying to talk to Adelle. She's not a bit concerned about the situation—Mother's death. You'd think at a time like this she'd give me some family support, not start entertaining, hardly the time to have someone to stay. All she's concerned with is keeping herself out of things. Like—where was she the night Mother went missing?'

Annette said, 'She was out.'

'Oh, yes, "she was out", was she?' Margo mimicked, like a spiteful girl in a playground. 'Where? She's never out on a Wednesday night. She lives her life like a timetable, I know all her moves to the last boring minute. How does anyone know she didn't take Mother up to the Edge—'

Annette waited for Hunter to speak. He said nothing. Let her dig herself in really deep.

'I'm not suggesting anything. All I'm saying—Mother was in such a funny state, she could have told my sister to drive her up . . . I'm not speaking ill of the dead, but my mother's word was law, nobody argued with her. But Adelle wouldn't be likely to admit she'd *seen* Mother, would she? And then, well . . .'

'Lost her?' Hunter suggested tonelessly.

'Well, she could have just wandered off. And where was Adelle that night? She won't tell me, I had a hell of a row with her about it . . .'

When he had sat down, Hunter found himself facing a melamine chest on which were several flamboyant photographs of Margo's wedding. He changed direction imperceptibly, for relief, and stared at an alcove crammed with any number of unattractive objects, including a dead *ficus elastica*. What took his attention was the way its withered leaves began to move. Then he realised it was set before a smeared mirror (as his mother would have said, 'And how long since that's seen a duster?') and it was not the plant that moved, but a reflection in the mirror. Through it, he had an oblique view of the door; either he had not closed it properly, or it had opened itself, or been opened. Someone was standing outside, listening.

Ron? Wouldn't he be out at work, engaged in his dubious car dealing? It was difficult to make out anything in the shadowed corridor, beyond a bulk, the pale blur of a face, occasionally repositioned, presumably as whoever leaned closer to catch his—or Annette's—lower tones. God knows, Margo, sitting with her back to the door, was loud enough.

Annette was not in a position to catch the reflection; she gave him the briefest, puzzled glance as he let Margo ramble on. He made the slight sign she interpreted correctly as *keep quiet*. Deliberately or not, Margo—imagining she could divert them away from the accident by a lunatic accusation—concentrated, repetitively, on her sister's shortcomings, taking their silence for interest.

'. . . just as she wouldn't *tell* me if Mother had asked her to take her up to Edge and she refused. But she was so upset, those pearls were a family heirloom—'

The door opened wide, silently. Charmian came in, said in her flat voice to the back of her mother's head, 'Granny's pearls were in your knickers drawer.'

Margo leaned sideways in the big chair, half turned. She looked sharply from Hunter to Annette. 'I'm keeping them both off school, there's so much publicity about Mother's death, we need the privacy of our grief. They're so young and impressionable and easily upset. People have very little tact, you know, asking questions—'

'Your granny made a mistake about losing her pearls,' Annette said encouragingly to Charmian.

'I said that,' Margo snapped. 'They were here all the time, in her drawer, I told—'

Charmian advanced to stand staring

expressionlessly at her mother. 'They were in *your knicker* drawer.'

Margo laughed. 'Kids get everything wrong, don't they? Now, Twinkle Toes, what about doing your homework. Go on, off you go.'

Charmian, rock solid, spoke with self-justifying emphasis. 'I was looking for Tracey's *present* because *Dad* was waiting to drive me and Joey to the Gables *that Wednesday*, and you couldn't *find* it, then Dad said look in your room—'

'Charmian, you're giving me a headache,' Margo snapped.

'So I looked in your *knicker* drawer and Granny's pearls were—'

'Talk sense, why would they be there?'

'I don't know, you keep all kinds of things in there—'

Margo laughed again, this time with a frantic edge, said, 'What's Joey doing?'

Charmian considered her reply. When she spoke it was with the satisfied air of one who knew how far to go, had reached it, and on the way managed to have her say. 'He's playing with his new computer, you know he plays kids' games all the time.'

Annette said sympathetically, 'My young brother's the same, they think it's just fun, but actually it can be an intellectual stimulus or something.' She had a fictional brother whose age and occupation varied according to whatever she needed him for. Hunter referred to him as 'your elastic brother.'

Charmian stared blankly at her.

'Have you got a computer?' Annette persevered brightly.

Charmian turned her slow stare to her mother. 'Dad said I could have a telly in my room and I haven't got it yet.'

'No, well, he'll have to take you to choose it. Maybe tomorrow. You know how busy we've been. Now, go on, or you'll get nothing.'

Charmian considered advantages and implications, turned and plodded out.

Margo made to get up, said with an air of finality, 'Well, I think that's about—'

'The accident,' Hunter said.

'I've told you,' she sounded pained.

'No,' he was polite, immovable. 'You've told me about the circumstances, not about what happened.'

That was, she explained—after several false starts—because she didn't know herself. It had been such a traumatic time for them all. Her father, her mother, herself. And the weather, the rain—

They would, Hunter said unyieldingly, disregard the weather. Now. The accident. What sort of accident? Who was involved?

She had no idea.

'Your mother? Your father?'

Well, she'd already *said* that, she was being as helpful as possible, all she seemed to do was help the police. But still she had no idea. Her parents had always been much too upset to speak of it. Because more or less immediately, because of his stroke, her father lost his speech, and her mother had too much worry to bear and now . . . now . . . was no longer . . . A whispered pause.

Hunter said, 'A mugging? A car accident?'

If only she'd known, she'd have been able to help. She then, enthusiastically, began to repeat everything she had just said.

Hunter looked at Annette who said, 'You did some pretty vigorous car cleaning the next morning. And in the house there was some bloodstained clothing—'

'Who told you that? Oh, yes,' confident, knowing. 'It could only have been Betty Rowle. Well, if you want to trust the word of a cleaning woman, not exactly known for her honesty. She's always been jealous of our position, it's her way of—'

They listened, stoically, Annette ostentatiously made notes. Realising this, Margo ran down, dried up. They regarded her in silence. Her eyes darted, avoiding contact and she began a garbled account of an accident her parents had witnessed and stopped to help—that was how they'd come to have blood all over their clothes. But not wishing to be involved they left before an ambulance arrived.

'Didn't it occur to you they might have caused an accident?'

'I looked, of course I did. I went over that car with a toothcomb, while they were at the hospital. It wasn't dented or anything.' A rapped-out, startlingly direct response, lapsing to the appealing, 'And just wanting to *help* I cleaned it out, just—to remove unpleasant reminders—'

'What else did you remove?'

She stared at them, her mouth open, then began to speak rapidly, 'It was Adelle's suggestion. I was too upset to think straight. Everything that happened then is just a blur to me. But I remember she said, if anything was—well—questionable—we had to protect them, and the family name, just in case, two frail old people—confused and not able to help themselves—one already with a possibly fatal condition, so it made sense to, if there was anything—'

'What did you remove from the car?'

For once a straight look: transparent honesty, wide eyes. 'I don't know. Something wrapped in a rug on the back seat. I didn't look at it, I just put the whole thing in a bin liner.'

'Where is it?'

'Adelle's, of course. I couldn't have it anywhere about here, it would upset my mother if she came on it. And she had *so* much to bear, so bravely. And it was up to Adelle to lend a *bit* of support, so I just did as she said. She's the clever, calculating one. I'm just instinctive, open, it just wouldn't have occurred to me to conceal—Not that I'm suggesting she *would* but she'd had all Ian's stuff hidden for ages—' She stopped, hand in front of her mouth, her small eyes staring above it, horrified at her own indiscretion.

Hunter stood up. 'Right, I think that's it for the moment. I'll let you know if we want to see you again, but we seem to have covered everything for now.'

To her evident relief, a sly hint of a smile, he made to go then paused. 'Oh, just one thing. A little while ago you made a serious accusation against your sister—taking your mother up to the Edge the night—'

'No, I didn't, I didn't accuse her. I'd never think such a thing. I'm so upset, even you have to realise when you've just lost your one remaining parent—it's very easy to say things that are confused and—'

'We'll see ourselves out.'

In the car, Annette said, 'Lying bitch.'

'Yes.'

'And trying to land her sister in it. Twice.'

'Yes.'

She looked at him, then waited, saying nothing. He checked the time, said, 'Drive me down to the town centre.' When they were there, he told her to pull up in a side street. The late afternoon comings and goings carried on around them as they sat talking. Margo showed all the symptoms of the classic liar beginning with the first small, entirely unnecessary lie about her mother going into the bookshop—reversing a factual situation. Trying to avoid mention of the accident, to the extent of attempting to put them off the scent by blaming Adelle for her mother's death. Charmian's catching her out about the whereabouts of Mrs Saddler's pearls. Her attempt to mislead them about the time of the accident. Her generalisations and irrelevancies, her aggression when questioned.

Annette said, 'But do you believe she really doesn't know about the accident?'

'That family never seem to tell each other anything if they can help it. It's possible—authoritative parents—why should they explain themselves? And if Margo had any sense—'

'Which she hasn't,' Annette murmured.

'True. But she's cunning. She'll make sure she doesn't know anything that might bring her trouble. She was sharp enough to think her parents might have caused an accident.'

'Trying to say Betty Rowle was lying about the bloodstained clothes. And playing the pathos card, what was it? Two confused and frail old people—they never existed. And now, they're spending money. Re-decorating. Computer for the boy, telly for the girl.'

'They might,' Hunter said mildly, 'be the kind of parents who spend endlessly on their children.'

'Come off it, guv. The trashy, run-down state of that living room. No, that's what we need to know, isn't it? Who gets the money.'

'There's the apparently independent sister and the errant son, could be any number of indigent relatives, but I'd say Margo. I think I can find out,' Hunter said. 'You go to the nick—' and he gave her instructions what to do when she got there.

CHAPTER TWENTY-TWO

It was Wednesday, half day for the shops that observed early closing. Rush bookshop did. Hunter had read the notice in the window on his first visit.

He had a rough idea where to find Mechanics Yard, winding his way through the oldest part of Rush Deeping where the sixteenth century timbered houses leaned their jettied upper storeys over narrow lanes.

Mechanics Yard had lost its apostrophe—perhaps over the years, perhaps it had never had one, from its beginnings a proletarian gesture of disdain to grammatical purists. It had lost its function, but the buildings of pale old brick remained: garages, workshops, stables, restored and redesigned, were set higgledy-piggledy, with small gardens or courtyards.

Dorcas's was number 5, paintwork rich deep blue and almond, light shining from the diamond-paned windows.

He rang the bell, the wonderful jangle-jangle of old corner shops. A shout from close within. 'Come in, it's open.'

She was in the odd shaped hall, on top of a rickety ladder, fixing a lampshade. 'You're always up ladders,' Hunter observed. 'Let me do that—that ladder doesn't look—'

'Done it,' she said triumphantly, came down too rapidly and had to jump as the ladder collapsed sideways.

He caught her, held her, fine-boned as a bird, snug in her big jersey. He could tuck her under his arm, carry her away somewhere.

She stepped back carefully, smiling up at him. 'I was beginning to enjoy that.'

'So was I.' *We must do it again some time.*

There was no polite formality in her smile, the warmth of her soft brown eyes, the delicate gesture of welcome. 'Come on in. It's—*chaos*.'

More of a comfortable muddle, waiting to be sorted; bookshelves and books were in place, everything else in boxes, or stacks, or making tentative claim on a civilised space. The kitchen was reasonably ordered; he kept her company there while she made tea. 'How did you know where to find me?'

'Never ask a policeman how he knows things.' On her desk at the shop, an invoice from a carpet firm, *Mrs Dorcas Grey*,

5 Mechanics Yard.

Half of the beamed sitting room was habitable, the fire in the old brick fireplace was laid ready, she put a match to it, took his British Warm from him.

They sat on the big, comfortable sofa, their mugs of tea on the low oak table beside it. A deep bookcase was fitted all along one wall, on its surface lamps and ornaments and photographs, a great pot of evergreen leaves. He asked about the photographs. The boy with her elfin looks and mismanaged limbs was her twelve-year-old son. The man beside him her brother, not her husband. 'Didn't marry me, the sod. Did a runner when I told him I was pregnant. My brother stands in as Dad, he does a terrific job. Dennis is staying with him till I get straight here.' She told him a little more of herself then asked directly, 'Why are you here, Mr Hunter?'

'Sheldon.'

She considered it. 'That's a nice name, it suits you.'

'The only Dorcas I know was the good woman in the Bible who sewed a lot.'

'That's not really me, more Adelle.' She made a faintly agonised face. 'I must say, it was decent of her to offer to stitch something for me. Cushions, things . . . but our tastes don't exactly coincide. I'm going to have to find some terribly polite way to turn her down. You haven't answered my question.'

She didn't have the vanity to think his interest in her could be personal—unlike her cousin Margo. Cousin. Could they be related? A funny, astute, thistledown woman and *Margo*? Honesty was the only course. Approximately, anyway. As for a personal interest, there would be another time, he'd already decided about that.

'When we were speaking to you in your shop, there was a . . . reticence.'

She looked down at her small hands, gentle, capable, clasped together. 'I felt it was all a bit—a bit dirty linen in public.'

'Not public—only me and Annette.'

'Is Ian in trouble?'

'Not with us, as far as I know.'

For a moment, in the candid gaze, a touch of cynicism. 'That's not saying anything, is it?'

'It's the truth. He might be able to throw some light on something that happened some time ago. You can't imagine how much time we spend following up enquiries that lead nowhere, this could be one of them. But we have to try.'

She said suddenly, 'He would never do anything illegal, or violent, or criminal. He was a sad person trying to make his way in life, always after some dream. I couldn't bear to think of you hounding him.'

'We're not, I promise. All we've done so far is to ask the few people closest to him if they know where he is, if he's all right. We haven't made any direct attempt ourselves to find him.' He spoke reassuringly to her for a while, aware of the ironic echo in 'people closest to him.' *A not very bright girl and her mother. A sister who doesn't want to know. And you.*

'Dorcas, you're one of the few people who knew of his interest in art. It may seem a silly question, but, did you ever see any of his paintings?'

'Why silly? My customers share all their obsessions with me. Art, they walk in here with sketchbooks, folios, asking my opinion. I sell some of their work—occasionally, I don't encourage that too much. But Ian, no. That's why I have wondered if it was all moonshine, I never saw a single painting—'

If she had, if it had had any discernible likeness to Casements, then, at the time, she couldn't have failed to recognise Fayne's work. Or—he checked the thought, she might have dismissed it as derivative.

She said, 'I did ask, God knows why, I must have been pissed. Would he like to show me some of his work? But he just clammed up. Said it was his personal vision and when I knew I'd be astonished. I'm still waiting. He's not in any danger, is he?'

'Do you have any reason to believe he could be?'

'Oh!'—exasperated. 'Stop stonewalling. I haven't set eyes on him for at least four years, how do I know what's going on in his world?

But when you last spoke to me you said that poor dumped girlfriend of his was worried about him disappearing.'

'Fair enough. She seemed to think there was something odd about it. But in view of what you told us . . . Did he ever bring her into the shop, did he bring any friends?'

'Sometimes, but not her, I'm sure—'

(Of course not. If Sandy had known that Dorcas was related to Ian, was a sympathetic listener, she'd have been haunting the place.)

'—from what Ian told me I doubt she could read. That's unkind, but they were completely different types. I couldn't help feeling sorry for her. They'd grown up together, it seemed she decided it was time for romance to blossom. At least, that's what he told me. He wasn't—he didn't—'

He waited, patient, communicative. She was going to tell him everything he wanted to know. Not everything voluntarily, but he'd get there.

Eventually.

'I have to be honest. Ian was a whinger. I suppose it's understandable, all things considered. He was farmed out to his Aunt Catherine in Chatfield when he was six, that's how he came to know Sandy. She was good enough for years as an emotional crutch. Someone uncomplaining, admiring, valuing him. Everything he's never had from his family. He used people.'

'Did he use you?'

'Yes. He never cadged, or anything like that. But, we were related, so I was a natural dumping ground. I *knew* how awful his father was, he didn't have to explain, or apologise.'

'Tell me.'

She told him of Ian's attempts to be reconciled with his parents, his disastrous moves back to Longley, the volcanic rows—very much as Annette and Mary Clegg had heard it from Betty Rowle. When he asked what exactly Joseph had had against his son, she shook her head. Joseph, as so many people knew him, never needed anything specific, he just needed confrontation. Ironically, he was driven to dictate Ian's life without giving a damn about him. And the rest of the family, too uncommunicative to make a concerted defiance even if they had ever felt like it, emotionally bulldozed, took their cue from him.

Margo literally turned her back on Ian because she knew it pleased her father. Adelle, in her own quiet way pretty formidable, was the only one halfway decent to Ian, but he was always insisting she take his side, putting her in the firing line. Eventually, she got tired of being used by Ian. 'He never knew when to stop. I suppose it was a desperation thing, really, everyone owed him something because yes, he had been badly treated.'

'But—his mother?'

A pause. 'I'm not speaking ill of the dead, and I really am sorry she met her end in such an undignified way. She was a matriarch, that doesn't necessarily mean she was maternal. You'd take her for a simple, placid countrywoman, but she was very manipulative, used her children as weapons. You know what Phillip Larkin said about parents.'

'Doesn't everyone?'

'Ian just kept making these—hopeless attempts to be reconciled with them. He could never grasp they were on totally different wavelengths.'

Hunter thought about that, it was interesting, and complicated. When he put it into words, 'Was that his way of getting their attention?' she said at once yes, that was it. If he had been what Joseph wanted—an obedient, colourless computer geek, they would never have noticed him at all.

But a maverick, forcing himself upon them, sending Joseph into a frenzy of bullying, giving Violet endless scope for outraged judgement, wedging himself between his siblings, causing embarrassment, scenes . . . Yes, Ian took centre stage. But at what cost? Sandy, dumped, callously ignored. Adelle set irrevocably against her father. Using Archie . . . Using Dorcas, confiding his current fad to her—the last direction she had called it.

The last direction—leading, inexorably, to Minim. The saddest cost of all.

He said, 'I'm going to ask you something very vulgar and personal.'

'How interesting,' she said with mischievous uncertainty.

'Another time . . . Does Margo inherit?'

She breathed, 'Bugger,' just audibly. Then, aloud, with a who-knows gesture, 'That's the accepted wisdom.'

'Any trouble about it?'

A sense of halting. 'Trouble?'

'Other claimants?'

She looked awkward, 'Oh, not—no. Well, rumour. Nobody's actually said anything.'

'Do they ever in the Saddler family?'

'Not if they can help it. It seems to come from the kids, so . . . for what it's worth.' She told him about Longley being put up for sale, Violet certainly not moving into the granny bungalow but possibly, just possibly, going to live in Canada. 'I don't believe she ever would have, frankly. And Margo felt entitled to something for helping with Joseph all those years. I can't think Violet would have let her down.'

'No,' he said thoughtfully. Checked his watch. 'May I use your phone?'

'Sure, it's in the kitchen,' She showed him through, left him to it, closing the door.

He asked for Annette. She was waiting for his call, ready with the information he wanted. After she'd given it to him, and they'd talked, she said, 'I've been checking road accidents-traffic for that date. There's nothing as far as I can see that's relevant.'

'Right. Did you tell Armstrong I need to borrow WPC Hart?'

'Yes.'

'Did he ask why?'

'Yes, but I told him I didn't know. And I don't, do I? Only . . . bits.' She managed not to sound accusing.

'Think it out.'

'I'm *trying* to. If only because James has been on the phone wanting to know what's going on.'

'Tell him what you know and take it from there. Twenty minutes and I'll be at the nick, all ready to go. OK?'

He went back to the sitting room, picked up his coat.

'Are you off now?' A fleeting regret. 'You could have stayed—oh, I know it's a tip.' She looked round helplessly.

'It's lovely. It's where you are you.'

'That's a nice thing to say. Are you trying to make me feel better about this . . .' She shrugged, her delicate hands outspread, offering up the gentle disorder.

There was a wordless moment. He smiled, took her hand, raised it to his lips. Then reached out, touched the silky warmth of her brown hair, alive against his fingers. The electric flare of interaction, sudden, erotic. 'Another time?'

She nodded. 'Yes.'

Leaving, he paused. 'Now, one question. What is it you really don't want me to know about Ian?' And at her expression—caught-out, cornered—'I might as well tell you, I pretty well know it already.'

CHAPTER TWENTY-THREE

Hunter cruised down Ruskin Close, WPC Hart beside him, checking house numbers. 'That's it, sir—over the other side. Eighteen.'

It was like all the other houses, well tended, gleaming, slickly smart in its fake rustication. The contrast to Longley House couldn't be greater. What they had in common was a complete lack of aesthetic appeal.

'Now I need somewhere to tuck us away—' They looked round, found a recess backed by a high, dark holly hedge. He drew into it, switched off his lights. Linda said, 'Look, the curtains are closed, but you can see the lights behind them. She's home already.'

'No, Annette checked. She didn't leave Chatfield till four-thirty—half an hour earlier than usual. That will be the guest she's got staying, according to her sister Margo.'

A pause filled with industrious thought. Linda said, 'Sir, if she's got a visitor, wouldn't she be at home with her, instead of at work?'

'Well done. Ergo, the guest was unexpected, Mrs Kenning didn't have time to organise any leave.' And as a skilfully driven Ford Sierra GLX swept into the Close and parked in the drive, he added, 'She's early. What's the betting the visitor's car is in the garage?' Because from what he knew of Adelle she was the kind of woman who scrupulously put her car away.

He murmured instructions, then with Linda walked quietly across the road. As the slim figure made for the front door, opened it, Hunter said, 'Good evening, Mrs—'

She gasped, spun round.

'Don't be alarmed. I'm DCI Hunter, this is WPC Hart. I'm sorry I startled you.'

'I see.' She recovered quickly. Whatever flustered her, she tucked it rapidly, neatly away. She had no choice but to walk through the open door, saying loudly, 'Heavens, I didn't think I'd have a visit from the police—' She managed to linger in the hall, slowly taking off her coat, depositing her briefcase, picking up her mail. It was some moments before she led them into the lounge. The lights were on, pitilessly bright; the aseptic room, needlework gorged, waited. Empty. The gas fire was lit.

Adelle stared at Linda, made no mention of having seen her before. She spoke to Hunter, 'This must be to do with Mother's death. Have you found out anything?'

Hunter said blandly they were still waiting for the results of tests.

'This is to do with an associated enquiry, if you'll just bear with me.' She had recovered quickly, if Annette and Collier had not described her so thoroughly, he might not have known there was something askew.

He said, 'Shall we sit down. WPC Hart might need to take notes . . .'

'This is official,' she said coldly.

He smiled, 'It's my memory, not fair to ask this lass what was said and blame her if we overlook something. Much better she gets it all down.'

Linda—out of her depth, but coping—wondered why this clever, intuitive man was playing the heavy plod. Annette had said to her, 'Whatever, just go along with it. And don't be surprised about anything, what he values most is support.' *He can have mine anytime. If only he'd ask.*

He had weighed it up: door to dining room, then kitchen. Following Adelle in he had left the lounge door open, which gave him a view of the hall, a section of the stairs.

Imperturbable, he sat down, made himself comfortable, then asked the last question she could have ever expected. 'You had the tenancy of a flat in Brighton from March nineteen eighty-five to February 1986.'

'What? Yes.' She did not sit, she scarcely moved, standing rigid and alert before the gas fire.

'If you could explain the circumstances.'

She too obviously swallowed the retort, *Why should I*? But she wanted to get rid of him, and as an intelligent woman knew the only way to do it was to answer his questions. 'I was on temporary transfer. It was my divorce. I needed to readjust to single life, to distance myself. Space.'

He regarded her silently, with interest.

Tersely, she explained practicalities: selling the matrimonial home, dividing its contents. He nodded understandingly. 'Stressful, all that. But, surely, your family, at such a time . . .'

She regarded him coldly. She gave him credit for reading the permanence of the Saddlers' combat zones, or it was none of his business. Either way a reply was unnecessary.

'Your brother Ian shared the flat.'

'No. I let him stay for a short while. He was in personal difficulty.'

That made two of them. And the family not giving a damn. He could see that she and Ian, however distanced and possibly not even liking each other, would make common cause because they were made to feel valueless and unwanted. He looked openly round the room. 'I notice you have no photograph of him. There isn't one at Longley House, is there?'

'Why on earth should I? Have you got one of a distant cousin? Because that's about what our relationship is. As for what's at Longley, that's their affair entirely.'

'I understand your mother was distressed by the loss of her pearls. Did she ask you to drive her up the Edge to look for them?'

Her face for once showed expression: perplexity. 'No, no . . . she'd be more likely to ask Margo, they'd had a drive up to the Edge earlier in the week. I'm at work during the day. For heaven's sake, it's dark when I get home, what would be the point . . .'

'In taking your mother up there in the dark, exactly. But this is what your sister seemed to be suggesting. Because your mother had been behaving oddly saying she was going to come here for supper with you—and you knew of no such arrangement. She might have got it into her head to come round here and ask you to help her look for this family heirloom—'

'Margo had the *nerve* to suggest—'

'But, as you told my colleagues, you weren't at home—Wednesday nights you attend a craft club.'

She swallowed the frigid rage, looked quickly away from him. Nodded.

After a pause he said, 'But that night?' She did not reply, gripped her hands tightly together.

'In view of recent developments, as I'm sure you'll appreciate, I must ask you—is that where you went that night?'

She lifted her head. 'I was with a man. He's married. From my department.'

'Right. He can verify that—no, his wife needn't know. Now, wherever your brother Ian is—and no one seems to know—you have some of his effects stored here.'

'Well . . . um . . .' She fumbled, disconcerted by the change of topic.

'I should like to see them.'

She drew breath. 'These personal arrangements can be of no concern to anyone except myself. I cannot allow you to—'

'Mrs Kenning, I can get a search warrant. It will take some time, I will have to leave WPC Hart here to make sure, in my absence, no evidence is removed. I will also, in the meanwhile, have to send a patrol car. The flashing lights will, I regret, disturb your neighbours—'

She wasn't going down without a fight. 'Do you think you can intimidate me?'

'That's not my intention. Our prime concern is the events of the twelfth of February 1986. The night, you will recall, when your parents were involved in an accident, and your father—'

They were interrupted. Suddenly.

A woman walked in from the dining room.

Adelle's height, weightier. She had luxuriant blonde curls, too much make-up. She was smartly dressed in stylish, elegantly designed clothes—rather too tight, spoiling the well-groomed effect. She was bizarre in the ordered room, could not have been a more unlikely acquaintance of Adelle's, who would surely be offended merely by the notion of being seen in public with her.

As if in confirmation of this, Adelle, self-contained and fluent, became disjointed. 'Oh, this is—guest. A friend—staying. That is—'

'Hallo, Ian,' Hunter said quietly.

CHAPTER TWENTY-FOUR

It was to Linda Hart's credit, and something Hunter never forgot, that she retained her professional calm.

The woman who confronted them appeared to be on the verge of an emotional eruption. The fat quivering face, working lips, the look of hurt appeal; hands—the dramatic urgency of the clasp of those delicate white hands, their long carmine nails. Everything said, plainly as words, *My nerves, my nerves . . .*

'I'm *not* Ian. I'm Iris.' The voice deepish in tone, breathy.

'OK,' Hunter said, glanced at the shiny modern grandmother clock ticking away on the far wall. 'If you want to get your story in first, you'd better start now. We haven't got much time.'

The woman gave no indication she had heard. Her arm swept out towards Adelle. Iris obviously shared all Margo's theatricality.

'I can't let you accuse her—'

'Ian—Iris, *shut up*.' Adelle's cutting voice.

'No, they want to make a scapegoat of you. I know all about being a scapegoat.'

'Oh, for God's sake.' Adelle sat down and put her hand to her brow for a moment.

'You're the only one with the decency to take me in, to accept me for what I am. This is a watershed in my life, it's time I took my true place in the world, Mother is beyond hurt—'

'I didn't take you in. You gave me no damned choice. You never *went* anywhere else. Wait till Margo sees you.'

'That bitch has always tried to land you in trouble. With Father—'

'No, that was *you*.'

'Miss Saddler,' Hunter paused, continued to address Iris with scrupulous courtesy. 'I assume you're still Miss Saddler, you haven't married?'

Adelle made a faint sound. Hunter, unrelentingly matter of fact, said to her, 'Your brother has had a sex change operation and is now, officially, in some respects, a woman. Transsexuals do go through forms of marriage, it's not uncommon.'

Adelle had nothing to say. Hunter turned to Iris. 'Your sister is storing some of your effects. I want to see them.'

'Those up in the loft? What for?' Iris asked, torn between pained puzzlement and gratification of Hunter's recognition of her status.

'*I* don't see, either—' Adelle began.

'I have told you I can get a search warrant. It'll be much easier if we settle this quietly now.'

'Oh, very well.'

'Linda, please accompany Mrs Kenning.'

Linda went promptly, glad of something practical to do that might stop her relieving her feelings by yelling with disbelieving laughter.

With Hunter for audience, Iris posed: gesturing, moving, spilling out of herself, creating an atmosphere of inadvertent slapstick.

'What on earth do you want with that stuff? My art career's over. I've put it in the past. I mean, I'm a different person now.'

Her ability to state the obvious without irony was of a piece with her self-absorption. Whyever Hunter was there, or anyone was there—this was all about Ian . . . Iris. Such a staggering ego would have been more than a match for Joseph's bullying.

'The money you made—as Fayne—for your Casement paintings paid for your sex change operation.'

'Of course, that's why I did it. It was too easy. That crap merchant Dorian ffloyd pitched me into the headlines—without him it would never have happened. I just took advantage. Why not? That's what's so fake about the arts, I could have built a career on nothing. Oh, I had some talent, and I *could* have gone on. If Minim hadn't been murdered. It had all been his idea—the anonymity—well, that suited me at the time, but it generated publicity and he got his jollies all right. I mean, he got as much out of it as I did and after all, I deserved a helping hand. I wasn't a clapped-out old queen. I was on the threshold of my new self, my new life, it took courage . . .'

And after all, Ian—Fayne—Iris—had gone through all these permutations. Survived. Felt herself now to be deserving of sympathy and respect. There was a devastating innocence about such self-centredness.

Linda and Adelle returned, arms full. There were boxes and packages of various sizes and a folding contraption: a spiral bound A4 sketchbook and portfolio. In the course of his wearyingly long and unresolved pursuit of Minim's killer Hunter had developed a nodding acquaintance with all kinds of artefacts and aids. He had come across this workmanlike compendium before—it was only now, with his retrospective knowledge, he could see how it fitted with Fayne's lifestyle. How he could dispense with all the visible impedimenta of easel, palette, how he could work and move himself and the tools of his trade without fuss, anonymously . . .

Adelle made a business-like stack on a table beside the sofa. On another table Linda deposited a black bin liner, oddly shaped, bulging.

Iris pointed to the neat collection on the first table. 'Those are what I left with you.'

'Yes.' A gesture towards the bin liner by Adelle. 'This is yours, too, according to Margo.'

'No, it's not.'

'Well, probably Margo packed it. Anything she gets her hands on—instant wreckage.'

Of the four people who stood looking at it, only one had any idea what it might contain—and he was operating on instinct.

Hunter untied the string, there was no way he would touch the contents of the bag. Holding the plastic on the outside, he managed it down, spreading out, opening out the folds of a rough tartan car rug—

Until it appeared.

Iris said prosaically, 'Well, I never. That's where it got to,' reducing to mild interest the ferment of media obsession, the mystery, the myths, the speculation.

And here it was at last. In the stultifying respectability of Adelle's lounge.

The Man in the Fog.

Hideously damaged. To Hunter's mind, the physical impact of the violence of Minim's death—which he had personally experienced—had its second haunting in the broken glass, the smashed frame, the ripped picture . . .

It had been described to him, he had tried

to imagine it, but now, with the spoiled thing spread before him, he returned reflexively to the momentum of the event—the crime, the plodding investigation, the minutiae of day-to-day work. The eventual wearying defeat. Now, everything was gathered into this moment of insight.

It was perfectly simple. *The Man in the Fog* was the final statement: the retreating man was Ian's maleness. The half concealed figure in the shadows was the woman he was to become, witnessing the departure of the unwanted self . . .

A private view.

A very private view.

Iris looked at it, put her hand forward, said, 'Why? How?' Hunter said, 'Don't touch, please.' But she had drawn back before making contact. This was her past, this was something she had jettisoned along with her male gender and what she saw as the whole fraudulent edifice of the art world.

She asked, bemused, 'How did it get in that state? How did it get here? Adelle, what—'

'I have no idea.' There was perception behind the reserve, it was impossible for a woman so astute to miss the whisper in the atmosphere: *this is something significant*.

Hunter explored, handling only the outside of the bin liner, the nerve jarring sound of splintered glass accompanying his movements. He took out his pen, pushed the shards aside.

Iris said, 'Look—Father's old craft knife.'

Between the folds of black plastic, in a bed of broken glass . . . Bright and sharp bladed, it had had a lifetime's wear, its wooden handle smoothed to the familiarity of a craftsman's hand. The brightness still showed, here and there, through the rusty black stains.

Iris turned to her sister. 'What's *that* doing here, Adelle?'

Hunter said quietly, 'You recognise it, Miss Saddler?'

'Of course. Please call me Iris. I've known it all my life. Father made the doll's house for Margo with this. And all the furniture. He never made anything for you, Adelle, or me. But you upholstered the furniture for that selfish cow. *I* wanted to do it, I've always had a marvellous sense of colour and design, but he nearly went insane when I offered to. You let me help you, sometimes, secretly, do you remember?'

Adelle, looking at the knife, spoke distantly, from a past unwillingly revisited, 'It was making it mine, in a way. I watched him for months, painstakingly carving. I thought, maybe he'd make something for me . . . And then, we were never allowed to play with the doll's house, Margo told him she didn't want us to touch it . . .'

'Why is the knife here?' Hunter asked.

'I told you. Margo brought that bin liner, just as it is—oh, August, I think.'

Hunter said, 'Are you sure? That it was only August?'

'Well, I don't know the exact day but it was after Mother came back from Canada.'

'Haven't you had it a great deal longer than that? Since the spring of 1986?'

'1986? Of course not. Why would I?'

Iris, overlooked, put herself centre stage by saying triumphantly to her sister, 'I painted that. You never believed me about my paintings, you said it was all make-believe. Just because you're such a philistine you'd never *heard* of Casements. Well, there, that's the most *famous* one.'

'Oh, yes. In my loft. Is that what's famous about them? They're all broken up and distributed in people's lofts.'

'Perhaps the date will be more significant to you if I tell you it was just after your father's—' Hunter was interrupted by a bitter outburst from Iris.

'I never had any recognition from any of you, much less *appreciation*—'

Linda, speaking for the first time, said with steady courtesy, 'Miss Saddler, that's something you can both go into later. For now, Mr Hunter has something important to speak to your sister about.'

'My father's what?' Adelle said, direct, and then, on a second thought, wary.

'The night of your father's stroke. The night of the accident,' Hunter said.

She looked away, her face closed.

Iris opened her mouth. Expertly, Linda drew her away, said quietly, 'I do like this jacket, the way it's cut. I haven't see anything like it.'

'No, well you won't, it's my own design . . .

Hunter turned to Adelle, dismissing the outlandishness of Linda talking clothes with all the purpose she would put into calming a mad horse.

'Your sister, Mrs Duggan, told you that your parents had been involved in an accident of some kind.' She was uncommunicative, but not a liar, she preferred silence. He asked her again, with an emphasis she could not ignore: he wasn't going to give up.

'Margo gets everything wrong, she exaggerates—'

'What did your parents tell you about it—then, or later?'

'Dad never regained his speech after that night. Mother was a reticent woman.'

He waited. Linda had drawn Iris away to a mirror, where muted conversation was taking place.

'Look, I asked her if she was all right. Because I'd had this convoluted tale from Margo about an accident they'd witnessed and stopped to give assistance. I think. Mother told me to ignore it. The—episode—was over and done with, her concern was Father, and nothing else. And so,' she added, after a pause, 'should mine be.'

She'd had her orders: *Shut up.* For the sake of peace she was unlikely to persist. Hunter said, 'It was unusual for your father to drive at night.'

'Yes, his eyesight.'

He sighed inwardly. She was going to give nothing away, he'd have to dig like a navvy. 'Do you know why they were out?'

She shook her head.

'Your sister hinted . . .' he lingered.

Her gaze sharpened. 'What? What? Margo never does anything as subtle as *hinting*.'

'Did he drink?'

She repeated, 'Drink,' in a calculated way, looked towards a sideboard set with silver tray, decanter, bottles. Then, candidly, 'At home, yes, why not? Don't we all? I wondered that. If he'd had a bit too much while he was driving home, been responsible—but there were never any enquiries, repercussions. So it couldn't have been anything serious, could it?' The cool abnegation of responsibility, her ordered life unthreatened.

'Didn't you ask yourself some questions though when, immediately after the—episode—your sister brought this—' He indicated the bin liner which was looking increasingly bizarre, like some extravagant statement of conceptual art.

'I told you,' she said firmly. 'I never set eyes on that till . . . beginning of August. I had no idea what was in it. My brother's—Iris's—artistic activities upset my parents. I never let them know I had stored various—whatever—' she looked at the orderly packages, then the bin liner. 'But *that* no. I didn't even know it existed until Margo brought it here. Then I just put it in the loft, I didn't look in it.'

'Earlier this afternoon, your sister gave me to understand that it has been in your possession since 1986. And that it was your suggestion to bring it here.'

The possibility of being the centre of attention exercised a gravitational pull on Iris, who bore down histrionically. 'Whatever she's up to, she's trying to land you in it. But *why* is it here, Adelle? I can't work that out at all.'

Hunter said, 'Iris, where did you last see this, and when?'

'At Minim's gallery, of course. The night of the private view.'

CHAPTER TWENTY-FIVE

In the quiet close a car raced. Too quickly and skilfully for anyone except Linda to notice, Hunter rearranged the displayed contents of the bin liner so that the knife was concealed.

Outside, the car revved, halted with furious braking.

Adelle's head jerked, 'I know who . . .' And

her eyes on him, full of a weary, accepting intelligence, said *You knew this would happen.*

'Yes,' Hunter said. He checked his watch; this would be the time Adelle always arrived home—but tonight she had left her office early. To attend to her inconvenient guest? Hunter had had time to clear the ground, establish a working base.

'Now—' He gave them instructions, calmly positioned them to the accompaniment of a frenzy of knocking and bell ringing. Iris's threat to faint, to *die*, met with a brisk, 'Be quiet, stand there. Linda, next to her—' which Linda interpreted as *Grab the silly bitch if you have to.* 'Mrs Kenning, go and open the door.'

'What shall I say?' She looked harassed and, for once, human.

'Nothing.'

She said helplessly, 'With Margo I never need to.'

'Exactly.'

They waited as Adelle went down the hall, opened the door to a torrent of words. 'Listen, you've got to get rid of Ian's stuff—that bloody Sherlock Holmes is going to come round sniffing it out and if he finds it, we'll all be in the shit—you for hiding it, Mum and Dad for getting hold of it—And that fucking Dorcas is mouthing off about—' On a wave of industrial strength scent, Margo's vociferous progress brought her storming into the lounge. To a dead stop. She stared at them all, mouth agape, face flaring scarlet. Her gaze swept past Iris. Wrenched back.

Her recognition was instant. There was too much in common: the bulkiness, the large face and small eyes. 'You fucking freak—'

'That's enough,' Hunter stepped between them. Linda manoeuvred herself in front of Iris. Adelle stared, distastefully, away from everyone.

'Right,' Hunter said into the sudden quiet. 'I *have* found it. Now you can tell me how it got here.'

Margo spared a glance at the bin liner and its contents, vehemently pulled herself together, glared at Adelle. 'Ask her, she was hiding it—'

'I was doing nothing of the sort, I've been storing some of Iris's things—'

'*Iris!*' Margo yelled.

'—since I moved back from Brighton. You came and added that to them last August. For your own reasons.'

'Why would I do that?' Margo mimed strenuous incredulity. 'It's too stupid. You expect people to believe—'

'I don't expect anything. They only have to ask your daughter. She was with you when you brought that thing here. As you've obviously forgotten.'

Hunter observed loudly to Linda that it would be as well to make a note to ask Mrs Duggan's daughter for confirmation.

Margo pointed, shouted, 'I'm not having my children anywhere *near* that pervert—'

'Ms Saddler isn't concerned—' Linda began.

'I am, I *am*. It's *my* painting.'

'Yours?' Margo stared. What do you want with a broken picture?'

'I mean it's mine because I painted it.'

'You? Paint?' a sneering response.

'I told you Ian did,' Adelle said.

'You said it was a load of bollocks—'

'I can't recall using that expression—'

Linda wondered, for a moment, why Hunter didn't sort them out. Then she realised. He needed to do nothing except continue deliberately letting them interact: they would tell him all sorts of things simply by shouting at each other.

Iris chose to ignore any intended insults. 'Why *did* you bring it here, Margo?'

'*I* told Adelle—I was worried sick about Mother. Neither of you have done a damn thing to support me, you left me to cope with her when she came back from Canada—absent minded, wandering about, losing her marbles—'

'Not to mention her pearls,' Adelle murmured.

'She'd started roaming about Longley, poking into everything. If she'd found *that* it would've brought back that awful night—' Margo spoke on, carried away by a narrative in which there was no place for truth or chronology.

Iris listened, frowning. After several attempts to speak, Adelle raised her voice. 'Shut up, Margo, you're not making sense.'

Iris shrilled, 'You keep talking about the night of Father's stroke—what's that got to do with *anything*?'

Hunter said, 'It was the night Minim was murdered.'

She looked around, bewildered, half aware. 'Adelle—you never said.'

'Why should I? It never meant anything to me.'

'What the sod are you all talking about?' Margo flung down her aggressively large handbag on the sofa and, overcome by some physical or mental exhaustion, crashed down beside it. Adelle winced.

Hunter told them, unyieldingly, in spare words, about the stabbing to death of Edward Minikin at the Minikin Contemporary Art Gallery in Chatfield on the evening of the twelfth of February 1986.

Only Iris reacted, aghast, 'The night of my private view—Adelle, *why* didn't you tell me it was *that* night Father had—'

'I've already said. The name meant nothing to me—why should it?'

Hunter said quietly to Adelle, 'You knew your brother painted, knew he was going to have a special exhibition in Chatfield—and that very same night a gallery owner was murdered in Chatfield.'

She listened impassively. She was already put-upon, now an intimation of violence had invaded her private space. 'How could I work out *dates*? I was moving house, trying to put my life back on track—how did I know, or care, what was going on around me? It didn't matter. *I* mattered. Yes, Ian made a nuisance of himself coming and going in Brighton, exaggerating about everything. Quite frankly it all went in one ear and out the other. Then he just dumped his stuff on me and went off to Spain.'

'When did you hear of Minim's death?' Hunter asked Iris.

'Must have been a couple of weeks later. Out of date English newspaper. I phoned Adelle—' She looked at her accusingly. 'You misled me, didn't you? If you'd told me Mum and Dad had been out that night . . .'

Hunter addressed Iris, 'Do you have any idea where they could have gone?'

She shook her head, puzzled. 'It was supposed to be my private view, but they never turned up there. So, well, I don't know . . .'

CHAPTER TWENTY-SIX

Hunter told everyone to sit down, with such authority they did so, except Adelle. There was a flush high on her cheeks. She bent down and switched off the gas fire. It was only then Hunter realised how stifling the room was, how thick with silence after the click of the switch. Adelle marched to a chair apart from the others, sat stiffly, stared at an embroidered picture of a crinolined lady standing on a rustic bridge in an English country garden.

Iris, crammed into a small velvet armchair, looked withdrawn, as if searching for the answer to an inward puzzle. When Hunter said, 'Tell me about that night at Minim's,' she typically did not answer him, but took up her dialogue with her sisters—that loop of past and present, never-ending and twisted, with all the mysterious qualities of a Mobius strip into which she had disappeared as a man and emerged as a woman.

She began at another time, earlier that week in 1986, when she had been to Longley to see her parents. She spoke seriously, absorbed in herself.

'I was at crisis point. I had to tell them everything. It was time. I mean everything—my painting, how important it was. Not for itself but because of what I'd *achieved*. I told them I was Fayne. Of course, *they'd* never heard of Casements, either, I hadn't expected them to. I begged them to come to the private view—they'd have been able to see for themselves how successful I was. I told them about that first because I thought—well, I thought they'd be so proud of me they'd be reconciled to my gender difficulties. They had a right to know I intended to be at the gallery as a woman.'

Adelle spoke, with a gasp, as if the words were wrenched from her, 'You must have been insane even to think he—they . . .' The thought silenced her.

'I had to try, I had to be *honest* for once. No one in this family ever is. Well, I was. And it took guts, I can tell you. He was furious—but that was bound to be his first reaction, I knew he needed time, to adjust—that's why I told them a couple of days beforehand. And that day, before I left, Mother had calmed him down a bit and he said if he did come to the gallery, it'd be to settle matters, once and for all. And I clung on to that. You know how blunt he was, he couldn't express anything subtle. I thought what he meant was that they would come, and he'd settle his mind, accept me—everything.'

It wasn't stupidity, it was self-deception on a massive scale, Hunter thought. He could grasp that a need so deep-rooted could blind her to anything she didn't wish to believe—but afterwards, to stay so focused on herself she could see nothing beyond the event? Then, as she continued, he wondered if this was the first time she had gone step by step through it—and in the company of her sisters, who had their own withheld fragments, their own evasions and contrivances.

And here was one small truth, at last. Fayne *had* been present at the private view—as Iris, dressed as a woman, safe in the knowledge that no one would recognise her except Minim, who had supported her through every stage. The nerve it had taken, to appear so publicly as a woman, spent itself in ashes. She saw her parents' absence as a betrayal and could not grasp that the betrayal was of her own delusion. Frantic, terrified of losing her nerve in the public gaze, she did the only thing she could possibly do—confront her parents again as herself, as she truly was.

She drove through the lashed, distorting night, to find Longley in darkness. In a surge of hope she convinced herself that, after all, they had gone to Chatfield. Why else should they not be at home? They never went out at night, especially in such conditions, it would have to be something hugely important—and to Iris the huge importance of herself displaced everything in the universe.

Immediately, she turned her car to begin the journey back. On the Chatfield road some assertion of reason made her stop and telephone Minim from a phone box, convinced he would say yes, her parents were there. But Minim could only tell the truth; however gently, and whatever kind words he spoke, Iris either never heard, or certainly never remembered. Overwhelmed, she stood in the phone box, sobbing.

The phone call. Minim's assistant, Ms Prendergast—'Only someone who knew him would have noticed something had made him sad . . .'

'Did you go back to the gallery?' Hunter asked.

Of course not. There would be no point. The odd pathos of the monologue sharpened to bitterness. They weren't there, they never would be there for her. She would never ask them anything ever again, never see them again. She went back to her Chatfield house, packed, and drove off in the dark to Brighton, to Adelle. A long drive; it was doubtful, even in a normal frame of mind, she would give a thought to the inconvenience of turning up without warning in the small hours, expecting sympathy, a place to stay.

She had previously made arrangements to go to a friend's apartment in Spain. She brought the trip forward to the next morning. When she left a sleep-disrupted, short-tempered Adelle, they neither of them had the least idea of the tragedy that had occurred—in the heart of their family—the night before, two hundred miles away.

Once out of the country, she didn't read the news, just didn't want to know anything, just wanted to hide and lick her wounds. When, later, she heard of Minim's death, she knew her old life was finally over, her dream of artistic success had finally ended.

Her dream. Minim's life . . . That seemed to be incidental.

All the while she was speaking, Hunter unreeled the action through his memory, returned it to its starting point.'

Joseph, beyond reason, enraged, determined to 'settle matters,' drives with Violet to Chatfield—perhaps he has decided to confront his son after the gallery closes, wait for him outside? Surely yes, he would not hold himself open to public ridicule; certainly they arrived, by chance or intent, after everyone had gone. Joseph, familiar with Chatfield all his life, knew the terrain, knew to park at the footpath end of the alley, where no one was likely to linger and take notice on such a cold, teeming night—and where, fortuitously, the lights had been vandalised. What few people were about scurried unseeingly along beneath umbrellas.

The gallery was still open, empty of its rackety crowd. They walked in. What would the mere sight of Minim do to a man in Joseph's state? Here was, he believed, the person responsible for Ian's gender dysfunction, for starting him on that path, for encouraging his degeneracy—

The frenzy would take no more than a few minutes, he had been goaded beyond reason, he always carried his craft knife with him . . . He was a hulking man, Minim short and slight. It would have been impossible for Violet to restrain him; if she tried to intervene—or she had merely to stand by—her clothes, like his, would have been covered in the spurting blood.

And then, in the appalled aftermath . . . The reinstatement of something like sanity, a moment, perhaps, to grasp what had brought them there. They only had Ian's word, not knowing the convoluted situation, the ditsy make-believe, the hard-headed commercialism, anonymity propelling the entire event. Fame, Ian had impressed on them. Maximum publicity. Publicity. That word and all its connotations would burn itself into the language of the inescapable everyday: scandal, tabloids, television.

And the only link between the nightmare of that disgrace and their unassailable respectability was the painting—as far as they had grasped—with the name of Saddler upon it . . .

Then, the urge to get away from the nightmare colliding with the imperative to get away with it.

Calculation. The stillness at the eye of the storm. They had touched nothing—except perhaps the painting. Had Joseph seized it, smashed it? His fingerprints . . . ? If they took away this physical object, there would be no notional trail leading to them.

So the same impulse that took them there made them remove all trace of their presence, their connection.

Iris's voice had a suddenly sharp edge. 'Adelle—when I phoned about Minim—you just dismissed—you didn't listen. All you told me was that Dad was in hospital—'

'I considered it marginally more relevant.'

Hunter regarded Iris with mendacious concern. 'I suppose she does have a point, but I can understand you being upset your sister didn't consider your feelings.'

'Upset,' Adelle repeated coldly. 'Iris has never been anything except upset, it's what she does instead of getting on with life. I repeat, I never made any connection between her arrival at my flat—and I might tell you in the dead of night, unannounced, for which to this day she hasn't apologised—with an hysterical story about *another* quarrel with our parents. When were they ever not quarrelling?'

Margo, small eyes darting, mouth open, had been following everything, mesmerised. She made a disruptive movement. Linda, strategically placed, took her arm, reining back any pugilistic reflex.

'You told me he had his stroke *after that last row.* You let me think that it was my fault, that I'd brought it on—' Iris's voice rose. 'You took no notice that night when I told you how devastated I was they hadn't turned up—but *you let me believe I was guilty* of causing Dad's—'

'And is it any wonder I took no notice? Do you know what you looked like? Staggering in at God knows what time in the morning, with this—this—*drama*. You in your wrecked drag, your wig askew—'

Hunter waited, listened through an interlude of high voices, waving arms, barked, 'Calm down, both of you.'

Adelle responded first, she was a contained woman, the nakedness of emotion offended her. 'I apologise. Excuse me,' she said to Iris. The stiff reinstatement of Saddler reserve had an immediate defusing effect.

Iris, breathing hard, sat down, gathered herself, gave Adelle a shrewd look. 'You know what doesn't ring true? You not seeing the obvious. Me and Minim. You work in Chatfield, read the local papers, hear the talk. All right, at the time your life was all over the place, backwards and forwards to Brighton, but the case was news—big news, for some time. And you're such a clever woman—'

But Adelle, it was plain, could contrive to ignore anything that might connect her with the accident. Hunter had enough now to read her. She would not dare risk telling Ian; in his overwrought state he could do something disastrous like going to the police *because* he had been there the night of the murder. With his obsession for his sensational self in whatever gender, whatever role, it would not enter his thoughts that an admission of involvement could rebound, lead to discreditable consequences. He might very well find such an outcome in keeping with his flamboyant persona—but for Adelle the smallest social transgression was distasteful. A major scandal would capsize everything: her career, her privacy, her dearly poised Rush Deeping life, the family name.

Margo erupted, bosom heaving. 'Of course you're responsible for Daddy's stroke. You were sunk in filth. Art and nudes, degenerates, drug takers, scroungers—'

'You can't see it, can you, you stupid cow.'

'What? What?' Margo's eyes swivelled, as if she could find the answer anywhere except on her sister's intent face.

Iris said carefully, 'I can give an account of where *I* was that night, and I was nowhere near. But you—just what were *you* up to?'

'Mum left it all to me,' Margo burst out in one of her flying tangents. 'I had my own family to look after. But there I was, left to cope with Daddy all those years—and he was a *sod*. And never the faintest help from either of you. Adelle, with her *career*. You, with your disgusting operations . . .' She launched into a string of insults, repetitive and boring, like Margo herself, only to be brushed aside by an unexpectedly astute Iris—

'You haven't said a word yet that makes sense. Now's my chance to get it together, you've told Adelle all kinds of crap about that night—'

'I don't know *anything* about it. I was so upset—the state they were both in, two frail old people. And I had to handle everything on my own. I told you, Adelle—'

'Stop dragging me in to this. I was at the other end of the country, remember?'

There were three of them at it now. It was probably, Hunter thought, a typical Saddler fight, in which farce, spite, anger, selfishness, all played their part. There was a surreal sense that, in their hostility, they were for once united. He leaned towards Linda, said softly, 'The other two have been telling the truth—or avoiding it. That one's a downright liar. See if you can get on her wavelength, I can't, she has her own reasons for thinking I'm a bastard.' He drew back, his sea-grey eyes holding her gaze. 'OK?'

'Yes, sir.' The professional response of one half of her. The other half falling in love, totally, forever.

Adelle was watching. She was too fastidious to lose herself completely, or for long, in the raucous to and fro of her sisters, and too intelligent not to see what Hunter was doing. She spoke with the force of habitual authority. 'It's time we all calmed down.'

CHAPTER TWENTY-SEVEN

Linda said to Margo, 'I can appreciate the difficulty your father had in accepting Iris, as I'm sure you can, after all, you're a sophisticated woman. But he would never understand the artistic world—'

'Of course he couldn't,' Iris said excitedly. 'Neither could Mother. I *tried* to explain—how the new Casement would be unveiled *as mine*. It was my triumph, and I wanted them to share it. I mean, if anything, my success should have . . . reconciled them to me, impressed them. Appearances meant so much to them.'

Appearances. Hunter, looking at Margo and Adelle, realised that the crashing lack of irony went unnoticed. Couldn't they see just what Iris's appearance—her intended 'appearance'—might provoke in Joseph?

'I'm not going to sit here listening to this crap, I'm going—' Margo grappled her outsize handbag, made lunging motions from her embedded position on the sofa.

'You're not going anywhere,' Hunter said. 'You are a material witness, as such, it's your duty to assist the police. You are liable for prosecution if you withhold any relevant information.'

'Relevant . . . I haven't *got* any.'

'Oh, but you have,' Hunter said silkily. 'You've voluntarily admitted, in front of witnesses, that you brought that—' he indicated the bin liner, 'here immediately after it disappeared from the scene of a murder.'

Margo yelled, 'You're trying to trap me—'

Adelle, exasperated, said, 'Oh God, Margo, you always go too far, don't you?'

Margo opened and shut her mouth, sank

back. Just what she was material to, Linda didn't bother to think, she took up the sympathetic role. 'The sort of help you could give us would be invaluable. You see you hold some quite important details that perhaps you're not aware of . . .'

Iris, characteristically ignoring everyone and concentrating on one aspect of her life's trajectory, stared at the ruins of Casement Six. 'I still can't work out, Margo, how you got hold of this. And I'm entitled to know, after all, it is my property.'

Hunter said, 'It doesn't matter whose property it is, it's evidence that in due course needs to be placed before the Crown Court. As such, I have the power to seize it. Which is what I intend to do. WPC Hart will give you a receipt.'

Iris looked at it. At him. 'Evidence?'

'Minim's murder is still officially undetected.'

A pause. It was as if everything that had been said had carried them headlong towards this sudden stifled silence. The stillness on the edge of havoc.

Hunter looked slowly round, lingered on Margo, turned deliberately to Linda, nodded. *This is business.* His gaze went back to fasten on Margo, unsettling, implacable. 'Mrs Duggan. I want to hear exactly what happened that night.'

Margo rallied desperately, found a yah-hoo

voice. 'If you're such a brilliant detective, why don't you tell me.'

'For God's sake,' Adelle said with weary contempt, 'if you can't behave in a civilised fashion at least use what brain you've got. We can only tell him what we know, then he'll be satisfied and go away, you can clear off, and I can have a little peace in my home.' There was a change of note in her voice, fleetingly like a warning.

'Oh, shut up preaching. You know nothing because you'd never listen when I tried to tell you—'

Adelle gasped, 'You never told me *anything* that—'

Hunter said loudly, '*Now*, if you please, Mrs Duggan.'

Margo embarked on her self-vindicating story. To Hunter she was defiant; as Linda scarcely merited her notice she spoke to her inattentively, not realising how this gave Linda a chance to get under her guard.

Eventually, Hunter—dispensing with repetitions and irrelevancies and the monotony of everything repeated three or four times—untangled what he could from a narrative where fact, speculation and stupidly entrenched attitudes wove together a pattern that made a certain kind of sense. For the present, he settled for a general truth.

Margo arrived at Longley, the lights were on and her parents' car in the yard. She had to knock, ring, even shout for some time before her mother opened the door. She was shocked by her mother's distress and bloodstained clothes. Her mother said there'd been an accident and Joseph had only just made it home before becoming ill. She had got him to bed but he had got up somehow, and collapsed, unconscious, on the landing. She went back to attend to him while Margo telephoned for an ambulance.

The overwhelming event, the strain of driving in the dark, coping with the weather, glaring lights, speed, would inevitably take its toll on Joseph.

Violet was a strong woman whose bedrock was control, she quickly regained her balance, in spite of—perhaps because of—Margo, changed out of her bloodstained clothes, while Margo ranged the landing between her unconscious father and her mother's closed bedroom door, calling out questions and plunging towards hysteria.

Whatever the cataclysms of the night, Violet knew how to manage Margo, rounding on her for concerning herself with inessentials when her first, her only thought should be for her father. As for explaining why they had been out on such a night—why should she? Margo had no right to pry into their life; the accident they would speak of at a more appropriate time. Violet went off in the ambulance with Joseph and stayed at the hospital till the next day.

Margo, claiming a sleepless night, was up

early, distracted by the need to do something positive, to help. It occurred to her that her parents' car might be damaged and she went out to look at it. It was unlocked and the keys in the ignition, a sign of their agitation. On the back seat she found, wrapped in a plaid travelling rug, the broken picture and her father's craft knife; she could only think they were connected in some way with the previous evening, and knowing from experience that there were always two entirely difference versions of any one accident, decided to keep them. It was a spur of the moment decision, response to an instinct that her parents might require them as vindication. In order not to distress her mother at such a difficult time, she put the bundle in a bin liner and hid it one of the outbuildings.

There were no dents or breakages she could see on the car, but it was so badly mud-splashed she cleaned it just to make sure. It was during this process Betty Rowle turned up for her day's work. She was no help in a crisis, inquisitive and unhelpful, becoming hysterical about the bloodstained clothing Margo had collected from her parents' bedroom and put ready to wash.

When, later, Margo attempted to talk to her mother about the accident, Violet became deeply upset, uncharacteristically weepy, accusing Margo of taking advantage of Joseph's illness to bully her. Her behaviour caused Margo so much concern she questioned herself: was she being unsympathetic, expecting too much of an old woman under great emotional strain? And was it worth it simply to satisfy her curiosity when the situation, whatever it was, appeared to have resolved itself?

She knew by then that the bloodstained clothes she had hidden away would distress her mother immeasurably if she came on them by chance—so she burnt them in the central heating boiler. She was more concerned some time later to find Violet—who could not drive—fussing about inside Joseph's car. Margo asked her what she was looking for and Violet seemed to forget, muttered vaguely about 'leaving some things'. Margo, off-hand, afraid of precipitating something she could not control, said that she had tidied up, throwing away some odds and ends—an answer which seemed to satisfy her mother.

Their life continued, unremarkable until after Violet's return from Canada. She was in a funny state, wandering about the house, looking into corners, cupboards; when asked why she had no explanation. This, to Margo, was further proof of her deteriorating mental faculties. An added strain were the anonymous phone calls about Ian, the possibility they might revive memories of the accident and further threaten Violet's sanity. Margo considered it her duty to protect her mother—and, of course, her father's reputation. She was sure that if anything surfaced that might implicate them in the unknowable 'accident', then the evidence she had hidden away could be produced to support their story, whatever it was. But she was in a quandary, she could not keep the painting and knife at Longley in case her mother found them, and broke down completely—so she took them to Adelle.

So many questions bursting in the hot, enthralled room, and an overwhelming unvoiced scepticism: Margo's idiotic claim that her parents helped at an accident scene when everyone knew they would never in their lives voluntarily help anyone.

Iris said, '*Anonymous* calls? *What*, for God's sake? About what?'

'Ian, Ian. *You, you, you*,' Margo taunted savagely.

'You never told me about them,' Adelle said.

'Why should I? What's it to do with you?'

Hunter intervened. 'Your cousin Dorcas knew, from your children, as a matter of fact. I'm very surprised they didn't tell you,' he said smoothly to Adelle.

'They never see her, they never come here. Why should they?' Margo looked round contemptuously at the domestic perfection that so offended her.

Adelle said, 'How many more lies are you going to tell?' Her self-command slipped, displaced before the suspicion that Margo was trying to discredit her, push some obscure blame on her. 'You turn up last August, with that—thing, claiming it's Ian's, when he—

she—oh, *Iris*—says *nobody's* set eyes on it for four years. More. Since, in fact, the time you took it from Father's car, hid it—'

Margo said, superbly irrelevant, 'Daddy was always an aggressive driver.'

'Good God, you can talk,' Adelle breathed.

'Yes,' Iris said. 'How many of Ron's dodgy deals have you piled into lamp-posts?'

That they should be maintaining old battle stations when a terrible truth was shrieking at them amazed Hunter. Under cover of their noise he spoke quietly to Linda. She had been following like a hawk its prey, she had worked it out. 'Why don't they see it?'

'Because they don't want to,' she murmured.

Adelle, still needing to get even with Margo, pointed at Hunter, raised her voice, 'You told *him* that I brought it here after—'

'He would say that, wouldn't he?' Margo outshouted her. 'Haven't you heard of police harassment? How do I know what I told him, I was grief-stricken, not responsible—'

Iris said, 'And now are you trying to say Father was responsible for an accident? A hit and run or something? If their clothes were covered in blood, there'd have been blood in the car—but you didn't say anything about that. You, Miss Goody Two-shoes, hiding evidence '*to support their story, whatever it was*'. You weren't doing anything of the sort, you were looking for something incriminating—'

Thank you for clearing that up, Hunter said

silently.

'Iris, be quiet,' Adelle said, voice taut. 'Don't pay her the compliment of a coherent thought process.' She had collected herself; she had a logical mind, she could see the steps by which the past was beginning to trespass on the present.

Iris said, 'But . . . it was you who said she'd blackmailed her way back—'

Adelle cut her short, 'I need a drink.' She went to the sideboard. Iris, evidently puzzled, stood up and followed. Margo ranted. Hunter, unsurprised Adelle didn't offer anyone a drink, was surprised that she poured two glasses, handing one to Iris who accepted it wordlessly, as if this had become an established habit in the short time she had been an unwelcome guest. Adelle said something rapidly; on Iris's face a deepening bewilderment broke open to denial and shock. Linda was beside them in an instant, but Adelle, too quick for her, turned, composed, guiding Iris away.

Margo was stridently justifying herself, 'It would never have occurred to me—they were the most law abiding people in the world, you know that. How can you accuse them of—if it had been anything like that they'd have instantly reported—'

Ignoring her, Iris sat in careful, absorbed quiet, like someone recovering from a giddy spell.

Hunter said to Margo, 'You forget, you told me you went over the car with a fine toothcomb. My colleague will have a note of your exact words.' Margo gaped at him. He went on, 'You also said that *at the time* Mrs Kenning told you it might be necessary to protect your parents, the family name, in case there had been any wrongdoing, however inadvertent, so she suggested you give this—' he gestured towards the remains of Casement Six, 'to her, and she could hide it.'

Margo opened her mouth. Adelle's cold fury, perfectly enunciated, 'You lying bitch.'

'I *never* said that, he's made it up. I told him you already had some of Ian's stuff, so I brought that round here after Mum came back from Canada—'

'Mrs Duggan, I have you on record as saying—'

Margo made a floundering jump up from the sofa. 'Oh, shit. All you want is to make *someone* responsible for something that happened years ago. Well, you're out of luck, because whatever they did, they're dead, dead, dead and you—'

Adelle went up to her, spoke her name in a low, furious voice. She did not touch her, but there was an impression of physically manhandling her, and the contradictory notion that contact was repugnant. In the sterile discipline of Adelle's living space the two physical types were somehow shockingly evident, shockingly juxtaposed: one fragile, fastidious, the other sweaty, overburdened with flesh and scent. But there was no doubt, authority went to Adelle when it came to silencing Margo.

Iris said mechanically, 'Margo, you treacherous cow. This is how you repay them, is it? After you had it all—the spoiling, the attention, the treats—while we had to apologise for existing in the first place. Now you're trying to make out they were involved—'

Adelle faced them both. 'We none of us know what they were involved in, so the less we say about it, the better. If we let Mr Hunter ask us just what he needs to know, we can tell him, then he'll have no need to take up any more of our time.'

You're a cool, clever woman, but you're never going to be able to restrain your two barmy siblings. Nice try, though.

Hunter lingered, stretched the silence, looked at them in turn. Asked with fraudulent mildness, 'It must have occurred to you that the only place your parents went to that night was Minim's gallery.'

CHAPTER TWENTY-EIGHT

A cacophony, as he had expected: denials, accusations, Adelle's hopeless commands: *keep quiet*.

Under cover of the noise he spoke rapidly, comprehensively, to Linda. She nodded. He murmured, 'Like the porpoise in *Alice*.' She was momentarily panic stricken, finding herself pitched into one of his famously impenetrable non-sequiturs. Annette and James would instantly have recognised the Lobster Quadrille. *There's a porpoise close behind me and he's treading on my tail.* 'You're doing fine,' he said quietly.

'Mrs Kenning,' he raised his voice, and there was silence like a trap springing. 'You're wasting your time, they've said too much already. Anyone with half a brain can fit it all together.' Margo muttered something mutinous. 'Yes?' Hunter said with mild interest. She pressed her lips together, looked away.

Linda said to Margo, 'It's understandable that in the stress of the moment, you'd think all kinds of wild thoughts. You all knew how unusual it was for your father to drive in the dark. You were bound to wonder where he'd been—'

Adelle spoke to Iris, as if resuming an interrupted conversation. 'This is one occasion when it's not an insult to say Margo is truly totally ignorant. What can she know, Iris? She only does pyramid thinking. She's too stupid to read anything except trashy magazines, she's no patience with news programmes on TV, all she listens to on the radio is mindless pop music. As for the idea of connecting our parents with Fayne—with that—' Adelle studied the contents of the bin liner, shaking her head, 'No, that's totally beyond her.'

Iris made a distracted acknowledgement, her voice lost in the past. 'But they never turned up. They never went there at all. I phoned Minim and he told me.'

'They did, but afterwards,' Hunter said. 'Everyone had gone. Perhaps they mis-timed it, got held up.'

Linda said, 'You expected your father to go, didn't you? He said "to settle matters" and you thought he meant to settle his mind about you.'

'And wasn't I the fool?' Iris said painfully. 'But Mother would never . . . And he, I can't . . .'

Hunter said, 'Your father was a violent man, wasn't he?'

'Daddy would never have hurt a fly.' Margo took refuge in shouted clichés, stringing them with tedious lack of novelty along the same, endless loop. Her voice ran down beneath the gaze of her sisters. They had experienced, all their lives, their father's emotional violence.

Iris spoke on a sudden outpouring of bitterness and accusation, directed at Margo. 'And what about you? You had a broken marriage, no home for your kids, no job, nothing. And as far as Father was concerned, you could stew in your own juice. Then he's taken ill—*and what happens*? You're back in favour, *back in Longley*, and even your slimy husband is, too. And don't try and pull that one about Mother being such a frail old thing, going to pieces. Mother was mean and manipulative and tough as an old boot. Adelle said—'

Adelle interrupted, 'Whatever I said is strictly between us—'

But Iris swept on with driven honesty, 'It's time she realised we're on to her. You knew she'd somehow blackmailed her way back. That's what she used—my painting—the sheer uncertainty of where it was, what she'd done with it, would be enough to make Mother horse trade—'

'She needed someone to help with Daddy. Neither of you—'

'Of course she did. And she got you cheap.'

Margo snarled, 'What d'you mean—cheap?'

'You thought you were so clever, yes? Reinstated as the favourite daughter, you and all your family living rent free. What you got was years of acting as unpaid servant in that old dump, chauffeur, nursemaid, at her beck and call. Because she bamboozled you. Of course she told you she couldn't talk about that night—not because it upset her—because she dared not put anything into words that might give a sniff of the truth. If you'd had the sense to work the thing out, face her with it, ask her outright, you could really have feathered your—'

This brought an outburst of unintentional candour. '*Ask* Mother—face her . . . Don't be stupid.' Margo's awestruck voice spoke for them all, for their silent lifelong collusion: they would never dare challenge the matriarchal diktat. They were always helpless, always children, afraid of their parents.

Margo gave a desperate, half aware glance at Hunter, hissed, 'You realise what you're saying?'

'Yes,' Iris said. She looked at Hunter with a tragic intelligence that told him she was, finally, struggling with fragments of a dark, half guessed-at scene, finding her place there. If she had the courage to assemble all the elements of her skewed, denied, ramshackle life she might, finally, acknowledge this dreadful truth.

She would get no help from Adelle, who had the will and the tenacity to keep her face steadfastly turned from any understanding.

And he knew what they did not: how the past had been levered into the present by Sandy. Sandy, with her ludicrous pursuit of Ian, her anonymous phone calls and their galvanic threat of rediscovering an episode thankfully buried. Just, crucially, at the time Margo was being edged towards desperation about being forced to leave Longley; her mother's real, imagined or just maliciously taunted move to Canada . . .

That was why she took the painting and the knife from their hiding place and moved them to Adelle's. She would probably have gone on concealing them until she forgot what they were, just more junk in the junk-sprawled house—which on some future clearing-out would be thrown away; meaningless.

He was quite sure she had no knowledge—possibly not even suspicion—of the truth. The day after that calamitous night, alone to make her discoveries, when she came upon two baffling objects, bundled up with every indication of concealment, she answered to some calculating instinct, and kept them.

And as things turned out later, she could very well have congratulated herself on her foresight. Thinking that with the passage of time her mother might be more forthcoming she tried, indirectly, to draw her out, but met with a resistance that was more than the habit of domination. Familiar with all her mother's reactions, she knew she was exacerbating a difficult situation, cunning enough to recognise there might be some advantage for herself in it.

So she preserved evidence she could not make sense of and whose significance she never dared confront. It was all she had, nothing else—and if her mother found and destroyed it, she would have no bargaining power at all.

Iris could see that, so, probably, could

Adelle, although she would never commit herself. But a change had occurred in the room, an overturned moment when words, emotions, denials had outrun themselves: an indrawn breath, *wait, careful, slow down*. It was an enmeshing of all the old uncommunicative habits, a concerted sense of shrivelling back from the touch of something frightful. No one said it, no one yet had put it into words: their father—aided, abetted, protected by their mother—had killed Minim.

The intricacies of family recognition and reconciliation would resolve themselves, or not, in their own way, they were not now Hunter's concern. Something else was: the death of the fearsome old woman who had made such a wilderness of the lives of her children.

He studied Margo with a calculation she misunderstood and countered truculently, blundering into his dangerous silence.

'You really ought to learn to do your job. Now you *think* we've done it for you, you can stop harassing us.' Suppressed triumph on her big face, red lips glistening, button eyes gleaming, she thrust up to him. '*You can't prove anything*. Here you are, piddling about with something no one even remembers, certainly doesn't care about, while a defenceless old lady dies and you haven't a clue.'

'I need you to accompany me to the station to make a statement,' Hunter said calmly.

She gaped, gathered herself, 'Don't talk rubbish. Do you know who I am? I've got standing in this community. Accompany you to—Go and get stuffed.'

'You have evidence I need to put before a court and if you don't co-operate and supply it voluntarily, then I'll ensure that the court subpoenas—'

'What!' She looked so disbelieving it seemed the habitual laugh trembled behind her astonishment, ready to crash out. She stared around for help, at her sisters, who stood shocked, staring back; at Linda, who was the enemy but might be a source of sanity. At last, bursting out, 'I haven't done anything, you bloody idiot.'

'You've admitted to cleaning out your parents' car, burning their bloodstained clothes. You could be open to a charge of perverting the course of justice and liable for prosecution—'

'But—I wasn't doing it deliber—I didn't know what anything was about—'

'There's only your word for that. You could, on the morning of the thirteenth of February 1986, have conspired with your mother in an attempt to alter the course of justice by disposing of evidence.'

Margo stood in choked silence. Adelle said expressionlessly, 'I understood the police don't pursue a murder case when the suspect is dead.'

So that's what you're banking on, is it?

Linda spoke steadily, 'Mr Hunter needs to establish that the man who committed the murder is dead. It is necessary in the public interest to write off an unsolved crime, rather than leave it on the books as undetected.'

Adelle said, 'You'd never get it to court.'

'We can apply to have it detected under Home Office Counting rules but we need sufficient evidence to prove who did it before it can be written off.' Nothing in Hunter's manner suggested that he was completely out of order, and enjoying it. He didn't believe Margo and her mother had conspired, Margo simply took opportunistic action, as always. Whatever Adelle believed, she would never testify against her clumsy, mendacious sister—not for Margo's sake, but for the family name.

Iris? Iris had no loyalty to the family that had rejected her, no concern for its good reputation—and at the time of the murder she had been twenty-five miles away, all she could swear to was that Minim had been alive the last time she saw him. She had not heard of his murder until two weeks later, and in the years afterwards, when she occasionally returned to England, she would phone Adelle with news of her own progress. Not family news, all her striving to be reconciled with her parents had turned to hate; she was building a new life, in her own words 'emerging from the chrysalis'.

Then Joseph died. She had never put aside

the burden of guilt that she had caused his final illness; manoeuvred by Adelle, she decided against attending his funeral, certain her mother would not want her. Violet had never wanted either of them, ironically giving them cause for commiseration.

'Right,' Hunter said decisively, 'Iris, Mrs Kenning, you'll be required to confirm what was said here tonight. I'll arrange for an officer to take statements from you as soon as practicable. Now, Mrs Duggan . . .'

Linda had been holding her breath, wondering how long he could go on winging it. And she had had her part to play, too. It was, it could be said, an ensemble performance.

* * *

Annette sat in the driving seat of Hunter's car outside Rush Deeping nick, James in the back; off duty, he'd cadged a lift in a patrol car from Chatfield. 'How did you know something was coming up?' she asked.

'My whiskers twitched.' He tried to sound casual.

Knowing he was half dead with curiosity Annette repeated everything Hunter had so far managed to tell her. He considered. 'Margo. She's the one who threw her knickers at Hunter.'

'Don't remind me. She's giving a statement to Linda and Inspector Armstrong. But what's truth and what's fiction is anyone's guess. Everything she volunteers is suspect, everything's filtered through her own interests. What she's saying now contradicts virtually everything she said on our two interviews with her. But that doesn't seem to come home to her at all.'

'Well, inconsistency's a good indicator of guilt. And if you've got something as inconsistent as Ian—Iris—in your background, well . . .'

'That's pretty judgemental of you, considering.'

'Considering what? Have you seen me in high heels, frocks, make-up? Have you?'

'You probably go out after dark. Sorry, James, mistimed joke.'

'I'm a perfectly ordinary gay guy, at home with my ambiguity—if you must look at it like that.'

'But Iris—if it hadn't been for what she is, Joseph wouldn't have killed Minim. That's a heavy burden to carry, as well as everything else.'

'Yes.' They thought about the implications of this, quietly, then Annette went on, 'Adelle's an ice queen, she has her own standards, but Iris has got a sort of earthy honesty, in spite of her absolute selfishness. She looks bloody weird, though. Don't they all?'

'Now who's judgemental?'

'Oh, all right. Quits. Er—who's going to tell

Sandy Ian is alive and well and living as Iris?'

'I'm bloody not. Still . . . Margo's coughed about cleaning their car and burning the bloodstained clothes. Wow. Hunter's got her there. Do you think she did for the old girl? And why now?'

Annette explained about the possibility of Violet moving to Canada, altering her will. 'It seems she could have said something like that to the kids, or they overheard her talking to someone else. Might have. The other sisters don't seem to know. Mr Hunter says she's always played the family off against each other. If that's what she was doing this time, she's paid a hell of a price.'

'All the same, he's *done* it, he said he would, no matter how long it took. He's got Minim's murderer. He must be all over coloured lights.'

Annette gazed through the windscreen at the approach of Hunter's unmistakable bulk. 'Mmm. He seems a bit . . . I don't know. Calculating. He's up to something.'

Hunter got in the car, unsurprised to find James there, said pleasantly, 'Homing device?'

Annette asked warily, 'Everything all right, guv?'

'Just tying up some loose ends.'

James stopped trying to control his enthusiasm, said it was great about Minim, and various other jubilant things. 'Do you think Margo and her mother were messing with the evidence?'

'No. If the mother had been anywhere in it, it'd have been a decent job. Margo acted alone, impulsively, eye to the main chance even though she didn't know what it was.'

James said, puzzled, 'Then why are you leaning on her, guv?'

'She'll do everything she can to prove how co-operative she is, and she can tell us plenty that'll help clear a lot of unanswered questions. She'll be completely honest—as far as she knows what that means—so that she can concentrate her brain—what there is of it—and cunning to get off the charge of doing her mother in.'

'Did she?' Annette asked.

'I'm damned sure she did. But short of someone seeing her drive up to the Edge, or push the old girl over, short of her confessing or Ron spilling the beans, we'll never prove it.'

'Is Ron in on this?' James asked.

'What do you think?' Hunter said to Annette.

'I think the first thing to find out is what, if anything, he knows of the night of Minim's murder. He joined Margo at Longley very soon afterwards, I can't see her keeping everything to herself, she must have said something. Even if just to crow about her cleverness in persuading her mother to let them live there.'

'So? That was then—' James began.

'James, use your head,' Hunter said.

He thought for a moment. 'Right, yes. She could have told him something, it really wouldn't matter what, so long as it was just enough to make sure that if anything went wrong—at any time—he's implicated.'

Annette said, 'Yes. Now fast forward. Violet's death. What does he know about it—if anything? He didn't alibi Margo, he was at work while she was carting her mother about God knows where. She's a liar, not a good one, sooner or later she'll trip herself up. His instinct's for survival, he's got too much—everything—to lose now to risk being charged as an accomplice. So he'll swear blind, "It's got nothing to do with me, I didn't know what she was up to."'

'Then he can use—or make up—anything about Minim's murder as a sort of boomerang effect, to get himself off,' James said. 'If he gets away with it, it'll be more by good luck than intelligent action. You could get at her through him, guv.'

'Not me. I've other things to do.' Hunter fastened his safety belt decisively.

After a small, surprised silence, James said, 'We're not going after her?'

'What's the point? It'll take God knows how many man-hours and the contingency fund is already well outspent for that. And God knows what in sheer frustration dealing with that slippery pair. We've done the initial investigations and we haven't come up with any hard evidence. All we're left with is vague suspicions—which do not a court case make. I can't see myself wasting my time persuading Superintendent Garret to authorise any resources to continue. No,' he paused, smiled. 'I'll tell you what we'll do. We'll hand over to Inspector Armstrong.'

James looked at him, bewildered.

'Well, he's keen to prove what a high flier he is, let him get on with it.'

'Guv,' Annette said, with deepening suspicion and a desire to laugh, 'Have you been winding him up?'

'Winding him up? Me?' Po-faced.

'Yes. You. What exactly did you say to Inspector Armstrong?'

'What I said was what a feather in his cap it would be at his next promotion board if he was instrumental in turning a seemingly innocuous missing person enquiry—a seemingly intractable case—into a triumph.'

James, who knew Armstrong's bludgeoning drive, his lack of irony or humour, said innocently, 'I wonder how long it'll take him to realise you've dumped on him from a great height?'

'Don't be cheeky. We'd better be going, crime will be marching on somewhere, waiting for us to catch up. Annette, the sewing circle, and drive like hell.'